Dre...
REV...

For Sarah

Life being what it is, one dreams of revenge
— Gauguin

Dreams of REVENGE

Kevin Casey

Wolfhound Press

Published 1987 by
Wolfhound Press,
68 Mountjoy Square,
Dublin 1.

© Kevin Casey, 1977

First published 1977 by Faber and Faber

All rights reserved. No part of this book may be reproduced or utilised in any form or by any means electronic or mechanical, including photocopying, filming, recording, video or by any information storage and retrieval system without prior permission in writing from the publisher.

British Library Cataloguing in Publication Data
Casey, Kevin
   Dreams of revenge.
   I. Title
   823'.914 [F]   PR6053.A8/
ISBN 0-86327-112-X

This book is published with the assistance of
The Arts Council / An Chomhairle Ealaíon, Ireland.

Cover design: Jan de Fouw
Typesetting by Wendy A. Commins
Make-up by Paul Bray
Printed in Great Britain by
Richard Clay Ltd, Bungay, Suffolk

Chapter One

After all these months I have returned to the security of routine. One can build a wall with expected events and hide behind it, predicting the day; the time the alarm clock will ring, the time at which to go for the evening paper. This is, I suppose, the way that the old must use to make sense of dwindling time. There is no room in the carefully ordered day for the unexpected to happen. One could come to believe that even death would wait to find a place within the plan.

Guilt cannot last forever. It dwindles away like other and better feelings. There was a time when I believed that nothing could ever be quite the same again, that I was caught with guilt as another man might be caught in an unhappy marriage. I should have known that one cannot live that way, that the mind will not tolerate continual accusation. Excuses are made. Bit by bit I have extricated myself from moral blame.

This morning, I finished my book on Michael Davitt. The manuscript lies on my table like a memorial to buried guilt. I look at it with some pride. Less than a month ago, I did not believe that I could start work on it again. I was prepared to borrow more money and return the publisher's advance. Since then I have learned to forget as one might learn to betray; the process has been gradual. I have planned my days and worked and guilt has become just another memory. I can move through the past with some detachment now, to find, as in my book on Davitt, the events that really mattered.

I must start with that afternoon in Belfast.

It had rained all day and pools of water had formed in spaces on the pavements where stones had been taken away during some past confrontations with British troops. I had walked up Peter's Hill. Soldiers were guarding the entrance to Unity Flats and an armoured car came slowly down Shankill Road like an animal seeking food. I had been searched in Donegall Place, pressed against a wall as a soldier patted my pockets. He had examined my cigarette lighter before saying, "Right. That's all." I remember his worried face and the way he clenched his carbine as I walked away. I could not grow accustomed, I thought, to the sight and sound of soldiers on the streets, the nervous foot patrols and the rifles pointing from behind sandbags at the corners. They were there like threats in one's childhood, a constant reminder of fear and the unknown.

Some women were standing in a group on the pavement, looking across towards Unity Flats. A tricolour flapped from a window in a small, sad gesture of political defiance. It was ragged and heavy with rain. Then a hand appeared and pulled it quickly inside. "Those bitches," a woman said. She was wearing a threadbare coat and a strangely old-fashioned felt hat. "Those Fenian bitches! It's them that makes trouble for the rest of us, so it is." I moved away from them. I had learned to avoid the chance of conversation. It was no longer safe to be a stranger, to speak with a different accent. I went past the shabby shops with their broken windows and peeling, discoloured paint, the sodden bunting, the slogans scrawled across the gable-ends of houses. It might have been the Falls Road; the same dilapidation, the same decay. The slogans alone were different. The people had learned to hate in separate ways.

I watched a foot-patrol that was moving slowly along the opposite pavement. One of the soldiers walked backwards, looking up at the roofs where a sniper might be. Their camouflage jackets seemed oddly exotic, they hinted at the sun and at tropical vegetation. It was raining again and a smell of burning came faintly on the breeze. I am not a courageous man. My life has contained far too many deferred decisions, those small postponements that are another form of cowardice. I am seldom impulsive. When I heard the explosion, I wanted to run away, to run towards the city centre as if I could find some extra safety there. The noise was so frighteningly loud that its echoes went on and on like my confusion. Glass fell from a window above me and splintered near to my feet. A man ran quickly past, his elbow hit me on the chest and a car horn sounded like a scream. Then the echoes faded away and for a moment the only sound was of the rain beating down on the pavement. The kerbstones had been painted red, white and blue.

There was no point in running away. I realised that as I stepped across the glass and pulled up the collar of my coat in an effort to get some protection from the rain. There might have been other bombs in other parts of the city. No place was safe. I had gone to Belfast to experience that kind of tension. I had started my book on Davitt and thought that it would help my understanding of his theory. I felt very little, of course. Fear brings a momentary quickening of the senses, then all is the same. It would take some years in the city to understand life with the car that might explode, the package in the public house, the sound of shooting at night, the anonymous telephone warning. It was easy enough to visit violence when one did not have to stay, when there was a train that would take one back to safety that evening. I turned a corner and followed a small crowd of people to the end of a street. A soldier with a walkie-talkie stared at us. It was not difficult to guess at his fears. The radio was silent. He shook it and a voice rasped from it as if activated by the movement. As we passed him I saw relief spread like a kind of wonder across his face.

UVF Not an Inch Lynch. The rain beat against scrawled slogans on the walls. I could hear the bray of an ambulance coming towards us. The army had erected barriers and on an intersecting street the twisted wreck of a car was blazing like a bonfire. The wall of a public house had collapsed; rubble was piled high on the pavement. Dust swirled in the black smoke but I could see through it into a small bedroom. Its floor was sagging towards the street, the furniture flung in a corner. A picture still hung on one wall. As I watched, a table came sliding across the floor and fell down on to the pavement. A man pushed his way through the door. He seemed to be carrying a piece of meat. It was only when he fell that one saw that he was clutching what was left of his chest. "In the name of God," a woman beside me said. "Are they mad, are they mad, are they mad?" She was crying hysterically. Somebody led her away and the ambulances and fire-brigade arrived.

"You shouldn't be here at all. Go home," a soldier at the barrier said. "This is no place to be. There could be other bombs. Go home now, I said. Go home." "Ah, go home yourself," a man in the crowd shouted. "What use are you to us here?"

I was standing near to a painting of King Billy sitting, with a kind of stubborn confidence, on a horse. *Remember the Boyne*. The man who had come from the public house had been laid on a stretcher. When the firemen started to move the rubble they found what was left of a woman's body. They took away some bricks and her leg appeared like a detail from a nightmare one has had. A severed arm fell away as if it were part of the rubble. A fireman put it in a bag.

I turned and pushed back through the silent crowd. There was a Saracen in the street. I passed it, feeling an irrational guilt, and the soldiers stared at me without speaking. Black smoke from the burning car was passing above their heads. I walked towards the centre of the city. It had stopped raining but water dripped from roofs and flowed in gutters. A group of excited children ran past me. They were used to violence; they did not care. Their heroes fought at their own street corners, not on cinema screens.

"Michael!"

For a moment, I did not recognise Lawlor. I had never known him well. We had met in bars before he had gone to Belfast as a Northern correspondent. I had read a few of his reports and, once, I had heard him being interviewed on the radio. His Republican sources were good but his political judgements had seemed erratic to me.

"What are you doing here?" he asked.

I have gone back obsessively over this casual meeting again and again, attempting to remember each word, each trivial, meaningless detail. It had no importance at the time, yet I have returned to it in search of any significance as a scholar might try to decipher some marks on a stone for the hint of a civilisation. Nobody wants to believe that life is made up of chance leading on to chance, that they blunder into the future with missed appointments or casual conversations. It would be comforting to know that the choices one makes arrange the course of one's life, yet looking back I have found that only too often it is the accidents that have mattered.

If I had not met Lawlor then and arranged to see him later, would I have met Anna? It is a pointless question; I can never know the answer. It should not be asked. Yet it is the question that lay, for months, like a mine beneath the surface of my bitterness. If I had been on the other pavement; if I had left two minutes earlier; if he had not recognised me or had been in more of a hurry, would Anna be happy today? It has taken me all of this time to stop asking trivial questions like these and to find perspective; to go back like a traveller along the route that is marked out on the map, ignoring those blank areas where the journey might have been different and more safe.

Lawlor was going to see the damage that had been done by the explosion. He did not seem very concerned. "I gather," I remember him saying, "that it's not very much," as if he were talking about a child's bruised knee. He offered me a cigarette. "We've got a chap there already," he said, "but I thought that I'd come down just in case." It is often difficult to see the line between the professional and the callous. "You never know these days," he said, lighting his cigarette, "who might be involved."

I arranged to meet him at a quarter past five in the bar of the Europa Hotel. As I walked towards the sound of the city centre traffic, an old woman handed me a leaflet.

What is the SO CALLED SECRET of Fatima that the PAPISTS have never revealed? Did the WHORE OF BABYLON, the STINKING SCARLET WOMAN learn of her OWN DESTRUCTION?

The red ink was smudged on the cheap brown paper. Another line, printed in blue, read *JESUS will COME AGAIN in 1993.*

A security man outside the Europa Hotel apologised as he searched me. "It's all them bomb threats," he said, crouching down and running his hands along my legs. "There's been explosions before. You can't be too careful. It's not much of a summer, is it?"

To get to the hotel door I had to walk through a zig-zag line of barriers. It was raining again and a cold wind came up Great Victoria Street. Lawlor was waiting in the bar.

"You made it," he said, as if I had come unseen through enemy lines. I had been sick, leaning ashamed against the door of the post office in Royal Avenue. Later, as I drank in a small bar, my feelings had dissolved into pity and anger, those more acceptable variations of fear.

Lawlor bought two whiskies.

"Did you hear anything else," I asked him, "about the explosion?"

"No, nothing much," he said. "No one's claimed it yet. It can often take a while. They'll phone the office when they've made up their minds." He smiled, as if enjoying a private joke. "I was on to the hospital," he said. "Two men in the bar were killed and a woman who was passing by. Another woman is having both legs amputated." He might have been quoting a list of football results. "It could have been worse," he said.

"It seems bad enough," I said inadequately.

"It becomes quite relative," he said. "You have to draw up your own scale of working values. What other criterion is there? An explosion is either bigger or smaller than any of the ones that happened before it. Today wasn't like the Abercorn Restaurant and it wasn't a Bloody Sunday. Or a Bloody Friday. Would you like to sit over there?"

I followed him to a seat beside one of the windows.

"It's more comfortable here," he said.

I could see the security man waiting in his hut as rain came down like bullets against the barriers. An army lorry went past and a man ran for shelter in the doorway of a dry cleaning shop.

"Maybe you're right," I said, "but still, it does seem rather callous. When people are killed so pointlessly . . ."

"So what do you want me to do? Weep for them?" He added water to his whiskey. "That isn't the way that the news gets written. Reporters who get emotionally involved last for about six weeks here. Or become a mouthpiece for one of the organisations. I've seen it happen again and again. Only last week Mannion went home because he was convinced there were Provos under his bed, Provos in the boot of his car, Provos watching everything he did. That's more common than you'd ever believe."

I drank some whiskey and watched the rain come streaming down the window. Lawlor's voice went on like the other voices around us. The bar was becoming crowded. I remember having, for what seemed like several minutes, a feeling of unreality. The shattered house, the woman's mangled body were becoming oddly remote. It did not seem possible that they could belong in the same city as this comfort; the casual conversations, the clink of glasses, the insistence on life continuing as before. It seemed an indignity, like the mockery of a corpse.

". . . so what we want is the truth," I heard Lawlor saying. "Not what someone wants us to believe. It's a propaganda war. I'm up to the neck in invitations to lunch. Every day I read about twenty press releases and they all contradict each other with complete conviction. But I think I can draw distinctions between them which, with great respect, is more than can be said for most of my colleagues here."

Looking around the bar I recognised faces that appeared too often on television. One knew their opinions; it was easy to predict their reactions to any event. Each had a scenario for an easy settlement. Their reports were like college tutorials. The calm, clear voices went on behind the films of shooting and burning, analysing the new developments and pointing the way towards their version of a permanent peace. Many of the politicians – two of the most interviewed were leaning against the bar – were just as predictable. It was only too easy to grow detached and cynical and even bored with it all. One had the same conversations in bars; one exchanged, at dinner parties, the same safe views. The nightly horrors on the news could become just another television serial. I had seen acquaintances of mine move from emotional chauvinism to complete detachment. An ambivalent attitude to violence was replaced by an equally unhelpful indifference.

"You're not drinking," Lawlor said.

I finished my whiskey and brought the glasses to the bar.

"You're new here?" somebody asked.

"But I'm not Press," I said. The man smiled and turned away, excluding me from the club.

"Now Craig's an interesting chap," a girl was saying. "Yes I know, I know all about that. But still I find him interesting. Whatever happened to Bunting?" she was saying as I paid for the drinks and carried them back to our table. "Isn't he in Leeds or somewhere?"

I remember wanting to be a part of their club. A premonition of loneliness can be much worse than being alone. I knew that Barbara was going to leave me soon. The time for postponement was over. I could think of no new ways of holding her; there were no efforts left to make. I wasn't even sure, any more, if I wanted her to stay, and yet the sense of loss was as real as if I had loved her.

At some point, during the conversation, Lawlor mentioned his wife. I had not known that he was married.

"Oh, for nearly a year now," he said.

"Does she like it here?"

"She's in Dublin," he said. "There's no point in taking unnecessary risks. I get back to see her almost every weekend. She's a painter. Anna Ryan. You might know her work? As a matter of fact," he added, as if he had just remembered, "she has an exhibition coming off soon. At the Nassau Gallery."

"I must get to see it," I said. "They always send me a card."

"She's quite good," he said. "She sold the four pictures she showed at a group exhibition last year."

He was, I began to notice, a little drunk, a little more emphatic in speech and yet slightly less confident. He sat across from me like a schoolboy behind a desk.

"I'm not much of a judge, of course," he said as he looked down at his glass. "I'm rather old-fashioned. I prefer the representational. But that doesn't stop me seeing . . ."

He drank some whiskey.

"I'll certainly go to see them," I said.

"I'd like her to do well. She teaches art-classes part time. That's another reason," he said, "for her not being here. It's the price that we both have to pay."

He fumbled in his pocket as if about to produce her photograph, but took out cigarettes. "Oh damn it," he said as his name was called over the Tannoy. "That's probably the office now."

"I'd better catch my train."

"If you'd like to wait a few minutes . . ."

"No, don't bother coming," I said, aware of an awkwardness that had grown between us as if our conversation had been too tactless or too frank. He knew nothing then but later, like me, he must have regretted our meeting.

"We're very much in love," he said, surprisingly, at the door.

I could think of no reply. When, much later, I told this to Anna, she turned away from me and cried. That is how I think of her now although we were often happy in ways that, when I recall them, ring for me like jesters.

The station was beside the hotel. The passengers were already going through the security area. The glass roof over the platform had been blown away in some explosion and the rain came down relentlessly between the girders. I found a seat on the train and thought, unhappily, of home.

Chapter Two

I was going back to something in Dublin that I feared even more than violence. The train beat on towards the border; the low grey fields and the farmhouses went past and rain streamed down the window. I had not brought a book. Behind me, a group of men played a noisy game of cards. "Put it in the pot. Have you money? Put it in the pot!" I could hear the clink of coins on the folding table as I stared out at the rain.

That night I dreamed about a wet, grey landscape. A railway line stretched away between the marshes. In the distance, I could see the roofs of a town. I was standing on what might have been a footbridge, holding its iron rail. Beneath me, someone was shouting in a language that I did not understand. I heard what I thought was a train, but when I looked I saw that a crowd of people was marching up the line. The evening light had faded from the sky; black mountains were bulked beyond the distant town. The people were carrying torches. Light flickered across their faces and shadows writhed, like eels, around their feet. They were singing a song that was faintly familiar to me. A tall man was beating a drum. I remember my fear as if it had been real and the feeling of shame that lay beneath it. Then the singing stopped and a girl stepped forward and threw a plastic bag up on to the bridge. She stood there, looking at me. The people behind her were silent. I bent and opened the bag and found a severed arm, blood caked between the fingers. I remember crouching and staring at it as if expecting it to move although it was only half recognisable, like a piece of wood moulded by the sea. When I looked at the crowd again, I saw that Barbara was there, standing amongst the leaders, dressed as she had been on that first day outside the British embassy.

I thought of that day as the train beat on and the card players grew more raucous. The same grey rain had been falling on Merrion Square when I joined a crowd there and saw three black-draped coffins being left on the embassy steps. Steel shutters were across the windows. On the previous evening, after a Sinn Fein march from the General Post Office, the glass had been shattered by stones and by petrol bombs. There were scorch marks on the door. The guards who stood on the steps and along the path stared uneasily at the crowd. Much later, I heard one of them say to a man with a placard, "I'm Irish too." This was the aftermath of Bloody Sunday when soldiers of the Parachute Regiment had taken aim and shot thirteen unarmed men near Rossville Flats in Derry. They had been to a banned Civil Rights March; there were a few scuffles before the shots were fired. On Wednesday, a day of mourning, this crowd had gathered outside the embassy in Dublin for emotional revenge. I stood with my back pressed against the railings of the square. The overhanging trees gave a little shelter. Someone was singing a ballad. Beside me, a man held a black flag that flapped wetly in the cold February wind. "We'll show them," he said, "we'll show them. I never thought that I'd live to see the day." He was wearing a cap and an old tweed overcoat. There was no excitement on his face. "It's the only thing that they understand," he said, "with their bloody gunboats and their troops. You've got to use the boot on them.

There's no use talking. Did they ever listen to talk?" Rain came down along the flagpole and trickled across his thumbs. "Did they listen to talk in Aden? Tell me that. Did they listen to talk in Cyprus? Tell me that." The expression in his old, defeated face stayed strangely constant as his words grew more violent. "What happened in Kenya?" he asked me. "Was that talk? Tell me that. Was that talk? Could you call that talk? Was it talk that got rid of them out of here?" He gave a hoarse cheer as a petrol bomb smashed against the embassy door. "Now we're getting places," he said, waving his wet ragged flag. "Now we'll show them who's boss."

The guards left the steps and pushed at the people who were standing at the front of the crowd. There were shouts of protest. "There's Dev's police force for you," the man said loudly to me, "as crooked as he was. Look at that now!" More petrol bombs were being thrown and some men were shouting "Burn! Burn! Burn!" The embassy steps were covered with flames that leaped brightly against the door before dying away. "Come on! Come on!", the man said, "ye'll need more than bottles. Bring out the big stuff now."

I should have known that there would be a baton charge but it caught me unprepared. The crowd moved back and I was pressed painfully against the rusted railings. I felt them moving behind me. A woman was crying, holding up her badly bruised hand. Then the crowd began to scatter and people ran around the corner of the square and down by Holles Street Hospital. Two guards went past, holding a girl by the arms. There was blood on her face and she was shouting ineffectually and kicking at their legs. It was still raining heavily and smoke was coming from one of the embassy windows. I find that I remember these details much less vividly than the details of my dream. I was not afraid; the baton charge passed me by in seconds, like a gust of wind, and there was something like peace for several minutes before the crowd returned. Then the petrol bombs started to fly again. The frames of the embassy windows were burning. "Up the IRA," a man called. Nobody doubted the origin of the bombs, the carefully planned demonstration. "Burn! Burn! Burn! Burn!" the man with the black flag shouted. He was nearer to the embassy now but I recognised his voice and could see the flag flapping limply in the rain. The clanging of bells sounded like an ineffectual protest as fire-brigades were blocked by the crowd. Later, the hoses were cut. The desire for revenge ceased to be dangerous but theatrical and turned violent.

The guards came running hopelessly into the crowd, their batons raised above their heads. They seemed much more threatening than before; the charge was futile and indiscriminate. I saw a man fall and get kicked and a guard being hit with a piece of board on the back of his neck. When I tried to move, the press of people against me increased. Then a section of the railings collapsed. I fell back with it, my leg twisted painfully between two bars. As I attempted to release it, somebody fell on top of me, swearing against my shoulder. The pain in my leg was so sharp that I think I cried out. Around me, women were screaming and the sound of running feet seemed threateningly loud on the pavement.

The man who had fallen on me rolled away. "The bastards!" I heard him say. I was looking up, through the trees, at the dark grey sky and the rain came down on my face. I moved my leg carefully, getting it out from between the bars, and the pain faded. It was bruised but no bone was broken. I was able to stand and step out on to the pavement.

A girl was kneeling there, gathering the spilled contents of her bag. I found two shillings and a small silver phial. "This is my lucky day," she said, pointing to a broken umbrella. Rain dripped from her hair to a sodden blue denim jacket; her jeans were covered with mud. "I think that's everything." The streets were filling again with people and the guards had gone. When she stood beside me the top of her head barely reached up to my shoulder. "Did you get hurt?" she asked. "I very nearly fell back with the railings myself. Someone could have got killed." She spoke with an English accent. "Do you think that I ought to be here?"

"I wouldn't speak too loudly at the moment."

"As bad as that?" she said with obvious excitement. Her smile was as open as a child's. She brushed at the knees of her jeans with her hands and said, "It doesn't matter to me. They can burn it to the ground as far as I'm concerned. I didn't vote for Heath and I don't like the Paras any more than they do. It's just that it seems a bit pointless."

Her hair was plastered flat across her head and there was rain on her lips as she smiled.

"It's pointless to me as well," I said, "like most of what's happened in the North. But it isn't pointless to the IRA. It will look like real support."

"Are they here, do you think?" she asked, looking around, the excitement back in her voice.

"I saw Joe Cahill standing on a lorry. You can be quite certain . . ."

"I never saw them," she said, "but you hear such a lot about them. What are they like?" A man standing near to us was holding a placard on which a coffin was painted, the figure 13 on its lid. "Is there any way of knowing who's here?"

As if to answer her, five men wearing black berets pushed through the crowd and went up the embassy steps. Two were carrying sledge-hammers. They started to beat at the door. The crowd was silent. The hammers splintered through wood but the door had been reinforced. The sharp, metallic knocking echoed like gunfire around the square. A woman shouted, "Up the IRA! Up the lads! Up the IRA!" and gradually the cry was picked up in other parts of the crowd. "So there they are," the girl said. She balanced on her toes to get a better view. "You were right. I've seen them now." She was holding tightly on to my arm for support. "They look very young," she said, "though it's difficult to be certain because of the dark glasses. Like the Tonton Macoute."

"Very like them."

"Do they hate everybody who's English?" she asked. "Or just politicians and soldiers?"

Some months later I was to discover the calculation that lay behind the curious innocence and directness of her questions. She could appeal, like a child, to one's protectiveness with her air of vulnerability; she could also hurt with all the self-contained, innocent ferocity of a child. It was often difficult to tell how conscious she was of the effect of her words or her actions. It took me too long to see past the mannerisms to the strength of her resolve. She moved through her days like some obsessed botanist who would burn huts, slaughter whole villages, to discover a rare plant.

If it had been possible to tell this story without making

any reference to Barbara, I would have done so. I would have moved on from my first meeting with Lawlor to the time that I met Anna, as if a new section of my life had started there and the past was quite unimportant. But we are formed by the past and the months in which I knew Barbara were shaping the future. I would not have gone, impulsively, to Amsterdam if I had not known her. That journey had as much to do with the rescue of injured pride as with desire.

On that first day outside the British embassy I could not have realised the implications of our meeting. I enjoyed being with her, answering questions, feeling her body pressed against mine. We were both so wet that the rain had ceased to matter.

"Old chauvinisms come to the surface," I said. "It isn't exactly hate. It's inherited dislike. Vague feelings of wrong done and vague desires for revenge. And the sense of superiority that feeds all nationalisms as witness the British themselves."

When the men gave up the attempt to break down the door the silence was almost startling. They threw the hammers on to the blackened steps and stood looking up at the building. Then one of them began to climb, heaving himself up from the other's shoulders to a ledge above the door and to a flagpole where a scorched Union Jack was hanging. He pulled the flag down and taking a tricolour from his pocket, tied it to the pole. This brought some cheering, yet there was a sense of anti-climax. The crowd was disappointed. "Up the IRA!" The cheering started again like an incentive to the men on the steps. "Where have all the policemen gone to?" the girl asked. She was still balancing on her toes, one hand on my shoulder. "I don't see any of them."

"They've done all they can," I said. "The situation has passed them completely. They're right to cut their losses. They'd only provoke more violence if they stayed."

"But that's a bit scarey."

"Pointless violence is," I said. I had started my book on Davitt and viewed all violence that was not defensive as senselessly retrograde. I resented the private armies that forced their wills on the people of Northern Ireland and the politicians who justified them or tried to use them for their own ends, as this crowd seemed to justify the IRA with imitative cheers. For weeks afterwards, people would come back to the square to look at the gutted embassy, as I would look at the burntout shell of my relationship with Barbara, revisiting the scene with some embarrassment and a certain disbelief. "A bomb! There's a bomb!" someone shouted. The men ran quickly down the steps. "Watch out, there's a bomb!" There was a loud explosion and the sound of metal being wrenched. The front of the embassy was almost blotted from view by swirls of smoke. "They've done it now," the girl said. Her wet body was pressed close against mine, her blouse moulded to her breasts. "I think they've blown the door in." The smoke was clearing; we could see into the hall. "They have," she said excitedly. "They've done it now." Her excitement was almost infectious. As she moved against me, I wanted her more than I wanted safety or peace.

"I don't care," she said, as if attempting to compensate for her nationality. "They shouldn't have shot those men. They weren't armed, were they? Some of them were only boys. It's no use saying the French were wrong in Algeria but that we're right in Belfast. Or the Americans in Vietnam."

"Bloody Sunday was murder," I said, "but your parallels aren't very exact."

"They're exact enough for me!"

A petrol bomb exploded, a blue angry blaze, in the embassy hall. There was loud cheering as more bombs showered in after it and the building began to burn. The heat was intense; flames came from cracks between the shutters and sparks blew above our heads. The ceilings of the ground floor collapsed in a mass of red cinders. Some fell out on to the pavement and burned there. The crowd began to push back and we moved with them towards Lower Mount Street.

"Well that's that, I suppose," she said.

"You'll notice," I said, "that after they pulled down the Union Jack they put up a tricolour. Then they burned it. That's a fairly accurate symbol of what they're about."

She was not listening to me. She walked ahead, wet denim clinging to her body, her bag across her shoulder.

"I told you we'd show them." The man with the black flag was standing beside me. "You remember me telling you that?" His flagpole had broken; he held one piece of it like a trophy. "Wasn't I right?" His face was still expressionless; the old, sad eyes stared out of it like a rebuke. "To think that I've lived to see the day," he said with what might have been surprise or gratitude. "Things'll never be the same after this."

I caught up with the girl. "You can still feel the heat," she said. "It will probably burn for hours." Some sparks came swirling down near to our feet.

"Can I give you a lift?" I asked. "I'm parked in Fitzwilliam Place."

"Is that very awkward? I'd simply love to get home and have a bath. I live in Ballsbridge."

"So do I."

"Oh, then that's very handy."

We walked up Fitzwilliam Street. Away from the crowd. I was conscious again of the rain that had seeped through my clothes. The girl sneezed. "It really was ridiculous, I suppose," she said, "to have stood there for so long in the rain. But I wouldn't have missed it, would you?"

I remember the rain on her face as she smiled and the way that she held her head to one side as she looked up at me. Images like these burned through the jealous days.

"I work there," she said, pointing to an advertising agency in Fitzwilliam Square.

Her name was Barbara Carson and she came from Wimbledon. That much I discovered as we drove along Upper Leeson Street and down Wellington Place. The streets were deserted, the surfaces glistening as if with ice. The leafless trees stooped dejectedly. "I hope that I don't get pneumonia," she said. "I don't think that I've ever been so wet before in all my life." Rain dripped from the sleeve of her jacket and on to the floor of the car.

Her flat was in Wellington Road. "The basement. I share it with a friend. It's rather nice," she said, "the rooms are big and we have the use of the back-garden." There was a light in one of the basement windows. "My friend must be in," she said. "I'd ask you in for a coffee or something if I didn't have to take a bath."

"Will I phone you tomorrow?"

"Why don't you do that?"

I watched her running quickly up the path and fumbling in her bag for a key. She waved and I drove to my own flat in

Raglan Road with a feeling of expectancy, as if I knew that someone would be waiting there. The flat was at the top of the house. As I climbed the stairs I could hear the elderly woman who lived on the floor below mine, playing unidentifiable tunes on her old piano. She lived in a forgotten world; old tunes, old photographs of the dead fading on her walls, old courtesies exchanged when we met.

The first two chapters of my book on Davitt were spread on the living-room table. It had been commissioned by an English publisher for a series of topical biographies. He had first contacted me having read three articles that I had written on the Land League for the *Irish Times*. I admired Davitt greatly; his rejection of a violent tradition and complex evolution as a socialist made him one of the most interesting figures in the politics of nineteenth-century Ireland.

The text of the book seemed less important to the publisher than the choice of illustrations. "There will be no page without at least one block, some may have as many as three. I envisage also a number of full-page colour plates," he had recently written to me. "Think of the writing as a pithy commentary on the illustrations. It is our experience that this can give a living dimension to a book, make the past more vivid, even bring real interest to a story that is essentially dull. I like to think of our readers as an audience in a theatre. Once the curtain goes up we must do everything possible to hold their interest."

This had not encouraged me but the advance was surprisingly good. When added to some savings that I had, it made it possible for me to take a year's leave of absence from my job as a teacher. The future seemed simple to me that night. It held the chance of something like success. As the train crossed the border and slowed near Dundalk, I was thinking back to those groundless expectations, unaware that the future was again being formed, growing out of the darkness around me like the lights of the approaching town.

The card game was over. Some of the players had gone to the bar, swaying in the corridor, struggling to open the door at the end of the carriage. The two who were left discussed the IRA with cautious admiration, as superstitious tribesmen might discuss an erratic local god. A woman with a sallow face and prematurely grey hair, shouted at a boy who was asking too many questions. He beat at her knees with his fists. "Why can't I? Why can't I? You promised that I could!" She sat there ignoring him, looking out into the darkness, a nerve twitching at the side of her mouth. The symptoms of stress are usually small and sad; the broken matchsticks at my feet, the nerve that will not stay still, the question repeated again and again without hope. In failure, the mind is dragged like a victim towards obsession. I should have recognised my own.

My affair with Barbara lasted for a little more than five months. We managed to avoid knowing each other for most of that time. This was easy to do. I made no attempt to see past the smile, the flow of talk, the easy approach that simplified all the details of our lives. We were even quite happy for a time. I could invent myself for her, producing thoughts or feelings that were opportune. She would smile in agreement; she seemed to have no fear of deception, so I deceived, boosting my confidence with the conception of a new and better self that was never challenged. If she had been less ready to accept this image, less innocent, as it appeared, I would have made some effort to find out what kind of person she was. In other relationships, although probably no more emotionally generous, I was, at least, more curious, more concerned about the truth but with her, there was too much to lose. I accepted her like some statistical fact made out in my favour.

Her approach to sex was totally without suspicion. She took it for granted. We came back to my flat after our second meeting and went to bed. She always undressed quickly, leaving her jeans and sweater trailed on the floor, her underclothes by the bed as she lay waiting. She seemed smaller when she was naked; her body, although not beautiful, provoked a simple excitement by its readiness to act. This implies detachment; there was certainly some vacuum behind the skill of her hands, the expert movements of her body, but I did not realise this for a time. She seldom spoke as we made love. She expressed herself physically, as if the act had nothing to do with the rest of her personality. This separation brought an element of fantasy to our lovemaking. It was more direct and simple than I was used to, less fraught with things to go wrong.

My mind invented reasons for this to add to the excitement of my body. I did not allow myself to wonder what she was thinking for that would have risked the end of uninvolved pleasure and could have dragged me back to the more familiar world of doubts and guilts and dissatisfactions. Our relationship centred on sex; almost every other activity became peripheral, something to do or talk about before or after making love. She would seldom spend the night with me but when she did I would wake to find that my sleeping body had moved on top of hers. I remember some of these mornings, stroking her body until she would wake and move to take me into her, as the only times of unhidden curiosity. I suppose that she had, when asleep, an additional air of remoteness that prompted wonder. But this curiosity was unexpressed; we remained intimate acquaintances.

A few weeks after our first meeting, a bomb went off in the Paratroopers' Aldershot headquarters, killing seven civilians. We were having a drink in the Shelbourne Hotel and I read out the details to her. Something about the indifference of her reaction annoyed me. "Do you think it's more excusable," I asked her, "than Bloody Sunday?"

"I don't know," she said. "I don't care particularly. What's the point in getting worked up about something that you can't change one way or the other?"

It was, had I known it, an honest expression of the biggest part of her philosophy, despite the fact that she liked momentary excitements.

"It's just that kind of indifference", I said, "or tacit support that created the climate in which all this violence is possible."

"It's different when it happens near to you," she said. "Then it's real. But not somewhere else. When you actually see it you have a reaction. It's just an abstraction otherwise. It's not even easy to believe in it. Did you believe everything that you were told about Vietnam? Even when you knew how wrong it was out there, how often did you think about it? I'll bet you didn't go on and on about it, did you? Be honest. Tell the truth!"

She was wearing black jeans and a black sweater that day and her hair was tied up with a scarf. Across the table from me, a glass of lager held between her hands, she assumed a moral superiority that I resented.

"That's just the kind of superficial reaction you had when they burned the embassy," I said, too loudly.

We were sitting near to a window; the traffic from Stephen's Green went past, braking noisily at a traffic lights, and a waiter who was serving coffee at another table glanced over at us. She was not in the least offended. "All right," she said, smiling, "give me the authentic reaction, the official view, the one that won't be superficial."

"So that you can agree with it superficially?"

"Maybe. Maybe not."

"You do one thing well," I said, deliberately attempting to hurt her, "maybe that's enough."

"You mean that I'm a good screw?"

"I'm sorry."

"Was that what you meant?"

"I didn't mean anything really."

"No, tell me. I'm just interested. Tell me."

"I'm sorry," I said again.

"Be sorry if you want to," she said, "it doesn't matter to me one way or the other. We get on all right, don't we?"

She put her glass on the table.

"You didn't deserve that," I said. "I know that I get cross and boring about violence and the remark was rather cheap. I wish that I hadn't made it. So I mean it when I say that I'm sorry."

"Forget about it, can't you?" she said, smiling, as if she were indulging a child. "You're a bit of an old puritan, aren't you?"

"Am I?"

"You must be. Otherwise you wouldn't think the remark had any importance. Or you wouldn't have made it in the first place. I only wondered what you meant."

Looking back at that scene and the unprovoked desire to hurt her, I detect a subconscious unease; something ticking away behind the simplification and the pleasure. Later, when we made love, I was more gentle with her than usual and it was very good. If I had a hint then of anything wrong I put it quickly away and attempted to go on as before. She did not want to stay for the night so I walked back with her to her flat. It was a cold night. We stood and kissed at the gate.

"Like teenagers," I said, holding her tightly.

"I'll be twenty-two next week," she said. "Next Thursday. Is that very old? What age are you anyway?"

"Twenty-eight," I said, subtracting one year, a recently acquired deception.

"Then twenty-two's not too bad."

"I'll get you a present."

"Will you?" she said with surprise. "I wasn't expecting anything."

"From me?"

"From anyone."

It was easy to feel protective then and to forget the urge towards aggression. I selected aspects of her to put together to form an acceptable likeness, as a detective puts together the different pieces of an identikit picture. I walked back to my flat. Already, it seemed to be cold and empty without her. She had re-arranged the furniture and thrown out the rubbish that had gathered in the small kitchen; a scent in the bedroom suggested that she was still there, waiting for me.

I bought her a gold Victorian locket for her birthday. She liked it very much. It contained the faded picture of an angular clergyman with a weak chin and a large moustache. We decided, for some reason that I cannot remember now, to call him Sweet William.

"I'll always leave him in it," Barbara said, holding the locket in her hand. "The poor old fellow. I feel quite sorry for him. It may be his only hope of posterity. I wonder what his wife was like." We were having dinner in the Unicorn. It was early in the evening and only a few of the other tables were taken.

"It's easier," I said, "to imagine his sermons. They'd certainly be full of masculine exhortation and cold baths. He'd have to compensate, like he compensated for that chin with the moustache. I can hear him advocating the rugged path to the Lord."

"Yet somebody loved him," she said.

"You assume."

"Enough, anyway, to keep his picture in this lovely locket. What a pity that people don't do those kind of things anymore."

"I wouldn't have thought", I said, "that you . . ."

She laughed and it was not until the end of the meal that she said, "We haven't got photographs of each other, have we?"

"I don't like cameras," I said, truthfully, yet attempting to evade the implication of the question.

"I do," she said, "but we haven't got them, have we? When we aren't together, will you be able to remember what I looked like?"

"Of course I will."

That was less than truthful. Faces blur in my mind like complex geometric problems. I remember gestures more clearly and certain inflections of voice, yet I remember her face now as easily as if I were looking at her picture.

"I don't think that I'd like to be anonymous," she said.

"You'll never be that."

"You think not?"

"Never," I said, a hollow reassurance of the kind that I associated with the clergyman at whose picture she was again looking.

"Dear Sweet William," she said. I realised that she was getting drunk. She had not gone back to her office after lunch. We had made love, then visited three or four bars. She liked the Bailey and Doheny and Nesbitts.

"Dear Sweet William," she said again, "you'll always be my talisman."

"Will you remember?" I asked.

"Remember what?"

"Remember what I looked like."

She considered for a moment, the locket left open on the table.

"No, probably not," she said. "I never have."

Her frankness hurt me more than I would have thought possible. I waited for a few seconds, attempting to decide if this had been deliberate.

"Do you mind that?" she asked.

"In a way I suppose that I do."

"Really?"

"Well, you said yourself that you wouldn't like to be anonymous."

"Oh, that's completely different," she said and smiled as if she had heard a particularly pleasing piece of news. "I meant anonymous to someone when I'm with him. I don't mind what I become afterwards. Not in the least."

"Then why did you mention photographs?"

"Just curiosity, prompted by my friend Sweet William here. You haven't told me yet what kind of wife you think he had. I'd say almost certainly stout. She probably mothered him a little. I can see her brushing hairs off his shoulder and making him change out of wet boots."

I remained disconcerted for a while but I do not believe that she noticed. I helped her to build up a picture of a fantasy life in a rural parsonage. We must have looked as if we were enjoying ourselves, yet I was thinking of what she had said about being anonymous. It was far too accurate a description of our relationship to be accidental. I remember looking for other hints in things that she said, examining her words as if they were spoken in code, but they held no second meaning. And, very soon, I was inventing myself for her again and ignoring anything that did not fit in with the most simple interpretation of her motives.

In that conversation we both agreed, for the first time, that there would be an end. We never pretended to love each other, never, even in passion, articulated anything but a need. On one occasion, out of an old habit, I almost made some declaration of love but she stopped me, putting her hand tightly over my mouth.

"Have you slept with many men?" I asked her one evening, moved by some obscure jealousy of her past.

"What do you think?" she answered.

"Quite a few?"

"You could put it like that, I suppose."

"And you've forgotten all their faces?"

"Did I say that?"

"Remember? On the night of your birthday."

"It makes me sound like some kind of whore."

"Not at all. Why should it?" I said, while wondering if this had been my secret intention. By now, the small unanalysed aggressions were coming more frequently to the surface.

"Do you ever think of me like that?" she asked with such simplicity that I felt guilt as sharp as pain. We were watching television in the living-room of her flat. It was a large, dark room with travel posters on the wall, rows of paperback books on home-made shelves and some big, uncomfortable chairs. I tried to take her in my arms but she pushed me away.

"No, tell me," she said calmly.

We looked for the truth from each other so seldom that we had no vocabulary to use. When one practises easy deceit as often as I had done, it is difficult not to be awkward in the world of frankness.

"Never," I said, meaning it.

"I wonder why you hesitated before you answered."

"Did I? It certainly wasn't because I didn't know."

"Then tell me why."

I could have told her, I suppose, that I seldom thought about her in any detail. She was someone in my bed, she was someone who did not challenge the small fantasies and defences that made life tolerable, she was a wet smile in the rain and an escape from loneliness.

"It must be because I am, as you've told me, an old puritan," I said, pushing along through familiar escape routes back to the freedom of the simple and safe. She smiled and made us coffee as I stared at the images moving on the television screen. She would never agree to make love in her own bed. I had seen her room only once and was surprised by its bareness. It might have been unoccupied were it not for some clothes left where they had fallen on the floor. Her flat-mate, Margaret, was a tall, laconic girl who studied psychology. She chain-smoked, peering at one through thick glasses, preparing to disagree with a kind of bored assurance. I met her only three or four times and vaguely disliked her.

This was the pattern of those months; meeting her most evenings, going to cinemas or out to dinner, making love with her in my flat. I worked on my life of Davitt in the mornings, reading through newspaper files in the National Library and finishing three more chapters. The violence in the North went on like the garish details of someone else's nightmare. When bombs exploded in the Abercorn Restaurant in Belfast, two people were killed and almost a hundred were injured, some of them appallingly. I saw the carnage on the television news; the bleeding faces and the missing limbs. The death toll mounted each week like a national debt.

I remember political events as if they had been small parts of our affair. This is reprehensible but true; it was my body and not my mind that selected priorities. I know where we were on the day that Stormont was prorogued and on the day that Harold Wilson came to Dublin. These were backgrounds of violence and security precautions to me and not real events; we were secure with our own small violences. In April, the Widgery Report was published. I remember the day on which it was leaked to the Press not only for its set of unsatisfactory conclusions but for another incident that affected me more directly.

I had arranged to meet Barbara in the lounge of the Shelbourne Hotel. While I was parking the car I saw her coming around the corner of Hume Street. She was wearing a faded fur jacket and a long black skirt that trailed on the ground as she walked. She did not look over when I blew the horn; there was something unusually dejected about the line of her shoulders and her bent head. I locked the car and ran after her. She was waiting at a traffic lights to cross the street to the Shelbourne.

I came up behind her and put my arms around her waist. She twisted violently, pushing at me with her hands, looking up at me in fear. There were tear-stains on her face.

"Oh, it's you," she said, putting her hands into her pockets and looking away.

"Have you been crying?"

A woman stared at us curiously, then crossed the street as the lights changed.

"I might have been," Barbara said. "You gave me a hell of a fright. Let's go back to Raglan Road."

"Do you not want a meal?"

"I'll make us something with whatever's there. Can we go now? Please?"

It was not until we were lying in bed that she described the experience that had upset her. She remained as tense and nervous as she had been when we met; smoking her cigarette too quickly, one bare arm beneath her head, her breasts pressing their shape against the sheet. She had left her office early and gone for a drink to a public house in Baggot Street. She could not remember its name. "A small place," she said, "I think we were in there once." She sat at the bar near to a group of men and read an evening paper. They were talking loudly and rather drunkenly about the Widgery Report. When she ordered her drink there was a silence, then one of them came over to her and asked if she were English. The barman had gone to the other end of the counter. "But I didn't suspect, at first," she told me. "I could see that he was drunk. Quite an old man. The others were younger but he must have been fifty anyway. He wasn't at all well dressed. So I told him that I was, yes, that I came from London but that I had a job here now. Then he asked me if I agreed with the Widgery Report and I said that I hadn't read it. 'It's just a whitewash,' he said. 'Everyone knew that it would be. It spits on the faces of young lads that the British murdered.' So I said that I thought that the troops had behaved very badly and he called one of the other men over. 'Did you hear that,' he said to him, 'did you hear what this bitch thinks? She thinks that the troops behaved very badly. Behaved badly! After they've murdered thirteen Irishmen in the streets?' So I said that I didn't mean to make little of it and the other man said to leave me alone. 'Behaved badly,' the man kept saying so I started to get up to leave."

She stubbed out her cigarette and reached for another from the pack on the bedside table. I lighted it for her. "He sounds like a fairly typical pub drunk," I said. "It was just bad luck that you ran into him."

"I was going to go to Doheny and Nesbitts," she said. "I wish that I had. But I thought it was going to rain and the other place seemed so handy."

I was impatient for both the story and the tension to be over. I tried to touch her but she said, "No, please, not now. I stood up to go but the man wouldn't let me get past. 'We don't want the likes of you in here,' he said. 'Do you hear me now? If you have any sense in your stupid little head you'll take advice. Don't come in here again. You'd be better off back where you came from.' So I said, 'All right, all right,' and I really was afraid. He was leaning up close to me and he had wild eyes." She was staring up at the ceiling; the tone of her voice was almost monotonous as if she were repeating something that she had learned but had not fully understood. "The other man just stood there," she said, "without doing anything. So I said again, 'All right, just please let me get out of here,' and he said, 'Remember what I told you. If you come in here again you'll have the tits cut off you, so you will.' "

She was crying quietly; the tears ran down along her cheeks and I was reminded of the rain on her face. "I'm very sorry that this happened to you," I said, holding her, "but you mustn't take it seriously. You really mustn't. He gave you a fright but he was just some old drunk who decided to pick on you. That's all. Just forget about it now. You'll never see him again. Would you like me", I asked her, "to find the bar and see if he's still there?"

"No, no," she said, "I don't want any more connection..."

"Then just forget about it," I said, feeling shamefully relieved. It was several years since I had hit anyone or been hit. I remember being guilty about my relief as if I had betrayed her in some way. I held her tightly, saying reassuring things until we made love. She stayed with me that night. I woke to hear her crying; when I tried to comfort her I found that she was asleep. That was, I suppose, the most anonymous time that we spent together.

The decline in whatever there had been between us was inevitable but obscured. It was there, inevitably, in the small aggressions and the more important pretence, yet even when we recognised that there would be an end we did not identify its causes. We went on practising the small destructions, like insects whose incessant determination will bring a building down. Barbara recovered very quickly from the incident in the bar. The next day she laughed about it, saying that it seemed quite unimportant and I did not tell her that I had watched, silently, as she cried.

"He was only a silly old ass," she said.

"That's all," I said, perhaps too eagerly, for she looked at me speculatively for a moment.

"It was a horrible threat, wasn't it?"

"Don't panic about it."

"Oh don't worry," she said, "I'm not thinking about it." She was dressing, picking up pieces of discarded clothing from the floor. "I'm not frightened any more or anything," she said, pulling on her blouse. "But still, it was fairly sinister. I don't suppose that I've ever been threatened as crudely as that before. It was actually as if he knew and hated me personally because of some harm that I'd done to him. It wasn't just an abstraction to him. It was really hate. But I don't care now. I knew that he was drunk. It couldn't matter less. I've known some men", she added casually, "who hated me. But at least they knew me."

She spoke with a kind of self-satisfaction, as if describing loves that she had experienced.

"Why did they hate you?" I asked uneasily, groping for the cigarettes.

"The usual reasons."

"Are there usual reasons?"

"Not for me," she said. "I've never hated anyone. I suppose that I've never come across anyone who was really worth hating. Have you?"

She pulled on the long black dress, fastening a belt at her waist. "But sex makes some men hate you, don't you think?"

"I wouldn't know."

She came across to the bed, smiling and kissed me.

"No, of course, you wouldn't."

I remember watching her leave the bedroom and hearing the hall door being banged. I felt strangely humiliated as if being unworthy of hate was much worse than being unloved. I lay there resenting her. From the flat below I could hear the sound of a piano; some old nostalgic melody being played in commemoration of the dead days or a dead love. One's moments of self-pity are always ludicrous when recalled. They show one at one's worst; the defences down, the fantasies exposed. I got up soon afterwards and went to the National Library and did some work but when I considered her again it was with a new coldness.

Perhaps the incident affected her more deeply than I had thought. She seemed a little subdued. Watching her closely I became aware of the depth of her self-absorption. I realised that her acceptance of my own invention sprang largely from disinterest. Some half-conceived recognition of this must have been behind my growing aggression. I had been the anonymous one.

Once I watched for self-absorption, I found a surprising degree of ruthlessness. She was interested in her own emotions and used other people to provoke them; that was their only function. She sought reaction as other women seek love, but sudden fear must have been outside the limit of feelings that she could control. In the bar she had become the victim of someone else's ruthlessness and that must have surprised her as much as my growing insight embittered me.

I thought up small ways of hurting her. I became quite expert in the barbed, the wounding remark. Most of the time I did not know if she even noticed. In bed, I used her more deliberately than before, but nothing changed. She would smile up at me, her small body gripping me as obsession grips the mind. I had, of course, been no different than her but that was no consolation. Hurt pride makes one blunder on like a wounded animal, more cautious than before but much more deadly.

"You seem to be picking on me a lot," she said to me weeks later.

"What do you mean by that?"

"You know what I mean. All the carping and criticising. Is there something on your mind?"

I could still be moved to protectiveness. We were walking down Baggot Street; we crossed the bridge over the canal, passing the young, blonde prostitute who waited there each night, and stopped outside Parsons Bookshop.

"Am I carping a lot?"

She was holding my hand in a way that seemed as trusting as a child.

"I don't think that I'm imagining it," she said.

I knew, by then, that what had seemed like innocence was just another detachment. She could be direct and simple, even trusting, for she had no fear of the implications of any answer. There was nothing for her to lose; it was very easy to move on to new experiences. We stood looking into the bookshop window; Paul Klee reproductions, the poems of Patrick Kavanagh; and the sentimental side of my aggression responded to her hand, the slightly crooked part in her hair, the angle of her head.

"I'm sorry," I said.

"No, don't be sorry. That's not it at all. I'd just like to know why it's happening."

"No reason that I can think of."

"Are you sure?" she asked. "Then that's all right."

If she had pursued it further I might have felt more hope. We walked slowly back to Wellington Road. The late drinkers were coming out of Searson's and shouting at each other as they got into cars. Someone said hello to Barbara. I retain the impression of a beard and a purple shirt.

"Who was that?"

"Just a friend," she said.

She asked me to come in for a coffee. "I think Margaret's out," she said. "I don't see any lights. Her exams are coming up soon."

"I don't think I'll bother," I said.

"Well, please yourself," she said, smiling. "I'll see you tomorrow."

I went back to my flat and found a letter from the English publisher. He wanted a report on progress. "There is a very good chance that I will be in Dublin soon," he wrote, "and we can iron out any difficulties that may have arisen in the text. In the meantime, if you would care to send me some chapters I would be pleased to see them and advise you if the style is suitable for the kind of book — and audience — that we have in mind."

I had been neglecting the book. Too much of my time had been spent in thinking of ways of doing without Barbara. I knew that we could not go on for much longer, that I was destroying whatever was left between us, yet I still feared losing her. It was like the thought of defeat at the end of a hopeless battle.

There were days when I attempted to postpone the end and the loneliness that I knew would be waiting beyond it. I tried to hold her by acting as if nothing had changed, but I could not carry out the pretence for long; the resentments were too deep. She would smile or look at me curiously as if I were speaking in a strange language and I would slip back into accusations with a fatal ease. If she had returned these accusations or shown any real sign of being disconcerted by my behaviour, I might have changed. Her only reaction was occasionally to ask me if there was something on my mind. The weeks went past like this. Our feelings were like a besieged town; we could not hold out for much longer.

On the morning that I went to Belfast, I telephoned her office from the station and asked her to meet me that night at ten.

"I've been thinking," she said with irritating vagueness.

"About what?"

"Us."

It was noisy in the station. A porter wheeled cases by on a trolley and over near to the booking office a child was screaming.

"What about us?" I asked uneasily.

"It's difficult to talk now."

"Well, don't just leave me in suspense."

"I'll tell you tonight," she said. "That would be much better. We can talk in comfort then. Why are you going to Belfast anyway?"

"I thought that I'd told you." Someone had shredded the telephone directory; the pages were strewn on the floor. "I'm hoping that it will help with the book."

"Oh, the book," she said.

"Yes, the book."

"All right, I'll come round this evening," she said, "I'll see you then."

I am what I am was scrawled in pencil across the dialling instructions.

*

The child who had asked so many questions was sleeping beside his mother. I caught her looking at him with something like disbelief as the nerve jerked the corner of her mouth. The card players left the carriage ahead of me, laughing a lot, like people on an excursion to the sea, who were determined to enjoy themselves in spite of the usual disappointments. One of them said, "We should have dealt you a hand," looking back at me across his shoulder, and the others laughed, without turning, as if this were the punch line of an unusually good joke. My car was parked in the station yard. I drove around by the Customs House and down the quays on the opposite side of the river.

It was a warm evening. A man was standing on the deck of

a Guinness boat and the seagulls screamed threateningly around the warehouses. Three Spanish sailors stood disconsolately on the pavement, looking for girls. The huge gasometer loomed against the sky in front of me like an ancient fortress. I was tempted to pass it, to avoid the meeting that might have to be decisive, but I turned right and drove along the empty streets towards home.

Chapter Three

I waited for an hour, watching the Irish news on television and looking at a book. There was a brief report on the Belfast bombing; the limbs being put in a bag, the sirens and the pile of smoking rubble. Each time that I heard the hall door being opened, I stood like a sentry listening to the creaking stairs. It was during this hour that jealousy came into me like a cancer. I remember wanting her yet regretting the occasional efforts that I had made to hold her. I went into the bedroom and thought that I could detect her scent like mockery in the air. The light from a lamp post outlined a corner of the bed. I went back again to the living-room and attempted to read but, at a quarter to twelve, unable to wait any longer, I went out to look for her.

I walked along Clyde Road. A couple were embracing under one of the trees and a cat moved ahead of me, crouching into the shadows. I went down Wellington Road and saw that there was a light in the living-room window of her flat.

Margaret opened the door and swayed slightly. I could see a bottle of whiskey and a single glass on a table in front of the fireplace. She blinked at me and said, "Surprise, surprise!"

"Is Barbara in?"

"A bigger surprise," she said. "No, she's not. I thought she was with you. Would you like a drink?"

"No thanks. You wouldn't have any idea where else she might be?"

"How many beds are there in Dublin?" she said with a bitterness that surprised me. I was accustomed to her assurance.

"Won't you come in anyway?"

"No, I'd better get back to my place in case she arrives."

"Hold on a minute," she said, "I've left a cigarette burning somewhere. There it is." She came back to the door and said, "You were saying?"

"Nothing."

"Have you had a row?"

"Not at all. I was delayed getting back from Belfast." I felt annoyed and embarrassed at all that she might know or guess about me. "Barbara must have waited and gone on somewhere else," I said. "She might even be back by now."

"She's not the kind who waits, is she?"

"Well, tell her I'm back if you see her."

"I'm not her bloody secretary."

I could see a faint smudge of mascara under the rim of her thick glasses, but I did not want to know about her problems.

"If you don't mind giving the message to her," I said.

"Oh, I'll give it to her, all right."

She stood in the doorway until I had closed the garden gate. I crossed to the corner of Elgin Road and waited for some minutes at a postbox, fumbling in my pocket when a car passed by, as if searching for a letter. I cannot be certain now if I was waiting there in the hope of seeing her walking towards me and alone, or in the fear of having my jealousy confirmed. Margaret's questions seeped slowly through my mind. I can understand now that my reasons for wanting to hold her had nothing to do with love and only a little to do with lust. They were almost entirely possessive. I was used to her presence and to her acquiescence. Standing there, certain that I had lost her, it was easy to forget the depth of her indifference. The thought of some other man enjoying her was like the end of real love. I felt as betrayed as if I had given her something that she could take away and share with someone else.

A man came towards me, holding a dog by a lead. I walked down Elgin Road, then turned and went past my flat, looking up at the windows. I did not want to go in there and be alone, so I walked down Clyde Road again. The couple were still embracing under the tree. I felt a twinge of envy and then sudden fear that the girl was Barbara. I crossed the road and walked slowly past. They both gave me hostile stares and I almost smiled with relief when I saw the girl's immature face.

"I saw him passing before," I heard her saying. "Come on. We'll go somewhere else. He's some kind of kinky . . ."

There was no light in any of the windows of Barbara's flat. I stood at the gate, wondering if she had come back while I had been away. I did not want to talk to Margaret again and, suddenly, I saw the pointlessness of being there waiting foolishly. I went home, glad not to pass the courting couple on the way. When I opened the door I saw Barbara, sitting in the only comfortable armchair in the room, reading the *New Statesman*.

"Hello," she said, "when I saw that the light was on I knew that you must be back."

I closed the door and the relief at seeing her was almost greater than the jealousy. It triumphed for a few minutes, like grace, and then it was gone.

"When I went to look for you," I said, "Margaret was drunk."

"Yes, she's having some trouble," she said. "Poor Margaret, with all her psychology she's always surprised when somebody ditches her. Then she gets drunk and sits in the lavatory for hours."

"She didn't know where you were."

"Is there any reason why she should?"

I sat down opposite to her.

"You said you'd be here at ten."

"Yes, I'm sorry that I was delayed. How was Belfast?" she asked, as if we were making small talk at a party.

"Where were you?"

"I met some friends. Do you have to sound so solemn?"

It was cold in the room; each winter, dampness spread across the ceiling like a map. In summer, the outline remained like an unexplored region in an old atlas. I switched on the electric fire and Barbara said, "You're not all cross again, are you?"

"No, not cross," I said. "Just tired. You said on the phone this morning that you'd been thinking about us."

"Yes, I have been," she said. "Just recently." She took a packet of cigarettes from her bag and offered me one. "All right, tell me," I said, holding out a match. "I don't like spurious suspense."

"It's hardly spurious, is it?"

"What have you been thinking?"

"Nothing very important," she said. "It's just that things between us aren't exactly the same as they were, are they?"

"And, of course, that's not important."

"You're not making it easy for us to talk," she said, so reasonably that the sound of my own voice seemed to echo bitterness, accusing me as much as it accused her.

"All right," I said, "I agree. What do you want to do about it?"

"Well, I can't do anything if you don't, can I?"

I am groping in my memory for the words that we used. The scene has become blurred, as if I had taken too much to drink or deliberately forgotten. I remember trivial details like the fire and the cigarette, the way that she sat curled on the chair and the sound of my own voice going on and on like that of a stranger. The words are less easily recalled. If in moments of grace we are urged to accept what is true, conversely we create damnation by accepting the promptings of feelings like jealousy and fear. There was no simple truth in my attitude to Barbara; the mixture of a growing resentment and an egotistical need were obviously destructive yet I know that I should not have brought down the building with such a disregard for us both.

"Were you in bed with someone?" I remember asking.

"This evening?"

"Yes, this evening."

She did not answer. I looked around the room, unwilling to see the expression on her face. It seemed bare and cheerless; the big oak sideboard, the chairs that did not match around the clumsy table, the books in disarray on the shelves, the carpet with its worn patches. I wondered how I had lived there for two years.

"I don't think you've the right", she said, "to ask me anything like that. You don't own me. We've made no promises. I never asked you that kind of question."

I looked at her, feeling ashamed that all of my carefully invented self had been so easily destroyed. Her calmness made it worse.

"Let's end it now," I said.

"Is that what you want?"

"Of course."

"You're sure?"

"I'm certain."

"All right," she said. "If you say so."

It was like a moment of intimacy. We sat there, without speaking. It had happened too quickly.

"I'm going home anyway," she said, "on holidays. I'll be away for most of August."

"I hope that you have a good time."

I wanted to ask her if she had been about to end it but I had not lost enough of my pride.

"Do you want Sweet William back?" she asked, holding the locket between her fingers. I almost went over to her to take her in my arms.

"No of course not," I said. "At least he's a face to remember."

"Yes," she said simply. "He is. I'm glad to have him. I must be getting sentimental." She sat up straight on the chair. "It's never the same, is it? Ending something."

"I haven't had your experience," I said, for even then, when there was something like peace between us I could not cover my bitterness.

"It's not really experience," she said. "Just a progression. You think everything is the same and then you find a different piece. I'm always surprised to feel something different, aren't you?"

"Why, what do you feel?"

"I don't know. Just something new. I think that's a good sign. It means that I'm not old," she said, smiling. "I'd hate just to feel the same things over and over again. Like being married. No wonder so many women attach themselves like limpets to their children. It's about the only new experience left to them. My mother was a bit like that."

She took her bag from the floor.

"I'd better go," she said. "It's getting late. I'm sure that I'll see you around."

"I know that I haven't a *right* to ask you," I said, "but will you tell me? Did you sleep with someone this evening?"

"Why do you want to know?"

"Just curiosity."

"No," she said, "it's more than curiosity. Would it make you feel more comfortable or something?"

"Perhaps it would."

"Well, I'm not going to tell you," she said. "Why should I? You needn't tell me what you did in Belfast."

I was tempted to start the argument again but my pride was greater than my anger.

"All right," I said. "Goodbye. You'll be able to get home all right."

"Of course I will."

I listened to her footsteps on the stairs and the sound that the front door made as she closed it for the last time.

Then the house was completely silent. I went to the bedroom window in time to see her turning the corner. A car went past, I could hear drunken voices raised in song and a cigarette end came spinning from one of its windows like a tropical insect. I went back to the living-room and sat in front of the small electric fire. After about half an hour I began to be glad that I had ended it before she had.

That night I dreamed about her. The girl threw the bag with the arm up on to the bridge and Barbara was there at the front of the crowd. When I woke I knew that something was wrong. I believe that I reached out to touch her and then I remembered. My instinct was towards revenge. If hell exists it must be an endless state of jealousy, not of regret. I do not believe that any emotion is more corrupting. I lived through the next few days like someone damned to confront a perpetual distortion of himself, as if forever facing a strange, leering face in the mirror. I could not concentrate on anything that I attempted to do for more than a few minutes. I stayed in the flat for two days, then went out on the second night to walk through the empty streets and brood on plans that were becoming less and less realistic. I remember Herbert Park with the trees arching gracefully above my head as if I were on an avenue. I went up Beaver Row to the Clonskeagh Road. I could hear the sounds of the river and, from the distance, the mournful barking of a dog. A guard flashed his torch at me, then turned it off as if satisfied of my unimportance. I wanted to speak to someone so I crossed the road and said, "It's a nice night."

"It's a nice morning," he said. "Could you not get a taxi or what?" and his loneliness reached out to me like the beam of the torch. He was an elderly man with an unambitious face, a little lost in the city.

"I couldn't sleep," I said.

"That's a terrible thing," he said. "A friend of mine suffered very bad that way." He leaned against a garden wall. I remember nothing else of our conversation for after that break into clarity the confusion started again. I pictured another man making love to her with a skill that I had never attained. I resented not knowing where she was, not being able to predict or to dictate her movements. Possessiveness burned beside the jealousy and the sense of failure. I walked along the main street of Dundrum, past the shops and the locked church, and stood beside the traffic lights at the corner. They continued to change colours as if there were traffic there to regulate. I was full of self-pity which is, I have found, like guilt, impossible to sustain for long without some justification. I justified myself, coming nearer to the truth than I suspected, yet I still wanted to see her.

I walked home and went slowly past her flat. The windows were dark. A milk van came down the road with a rattle of bottles and the roofs of the houses were beginning to assume a new clarity against the brightening sky.

I went back to my flat and got some sleep. I dreamed that I was moving through darkness. I pushed and pulled at it, choking as it gathered a palpable force. When I woke it was a bright summer's morning. I had not pulled the curtains and sunlight came like grace into the room.

I went down to the hall and telephoned her office.

"No, I'm sorry," the receptionist said. "She's on holidays. Would you like to leave a message for her?"

"There's not much point," I said. "Do you happen to know if she's gone home to England?"

"I think I heard her saying she was going to, yes. Shall I say who called?"

"No thanks."

I went upstairs and started to tidy the flat. There were two empty whiskey bottles in the bedroom and a pile of books that I had taken from the shelves but had left unread. I made some coffee. As the morning went past I felt more and more ashamed of the melodrama of the night. I read the chapters that I had written on Davitt, embarrassed by their tone. They argued that his greatness sprang from a strict adherence to the rational, despite all the potent reasons in his life for choosing violence. The eviction in his childhood, the loss of his arm, the prison sentences; all of these could have drawn him into the confused ways of emotional reaction, yet he had thought his way with difficulty to a recognition of the inevitable falsifications in the traditions of the oppressed. I accepted his conclusions, but I felt like a drunk advocating the merits of sobriety.

Chapter Four

In the days that followed, the confusion of feelings began to simplify until only jealousy remained. It stabbed like a shameful memory whenever I pictured her with someone, making love. These images sometimes recur even now but they have lost their power to hurt. I come across them as one comes across some object discarded at the back of a drawer. They once had a meaning, now they are only curiosities.

I worked on my book every day, pushing it forward, paragraph by paragraph, as if responding to a challenge. I disliked the evenings most; the thin sound of the piano and the cheerless drinks. When the card from the Nassau Gallery came, I left it without interest on the table. I had bought a picture there several years before and ever since they had sent me an invitation to each exhibition.

I read Anna's name on the card some days later and felt a certain interest. The exhibition of her work was opening that evening. I was curious, so I decided to go. The two small rooms of the gallery were filled with people when I got there. One could hardly see the pictures. I looked for Lawlor, pushing my way from one room to the other but he was not there.

I saw some people that I knew and made conversation with them as we drank poor sherry.

"She's growing," one of them said to me.

"Is she?"

"Don't you think so?"

"I haven't seen them yet."

He stared at me, surprised. I have never mastered the nimble art of small talk. I plod clumsily onwards. A Northern poet said, "There's a certain wistful quality in the work. A kind of precocious angst." Looking at his mournful face I wondered if he were joking but he waited, staring at me, for an answer.

"Whenever I come to an opening," I said, "I have to come back to look at the pictures. The only impressions that I take away are the back of people's heads and the taste of Cyprus sherry."

"It could be worse," he said, taking another glass from a passing tray. "Are you here alone?"

"Yes."

"I've seen you around," he said with what could have been malice, "with a nice little girl. Who is she?"

Someone jostled against me, spilling sherry on my sleeve.

"Oh she's no one," I said.

"An aisling? She looked quite real to me."

"I'm going to make an effort to see some pictures."

"The man from the Arts Council, with his unfailing skill," he said, "has already bought the only two bad pictures in the show." A smile moved cautiously across his face. "You know Anna, I suppose?"

"No I've never met her. I know her husband slightly."

"You'll see her in a long white dress looking healthy but interesting," he said. "She's like a pre-Raphaelite portrait that went wrong."

It was a strange exhibition. The pictures were painted in several distinct styles. They might have been the work of different artists; one looked at the signatures with surprise. It was disconcerting to move from one to the next and see the expression of such an uncertain personality. A number of the smaller landscapes suggested Corot. The trees and sky and meadows seemed about to dissolve to join the rivers that cut across the paintings in a tranquil progress of blues and greys and greens.

In others a golden horizon etched out figures who were posed in a dark foreground. I waited for some people to move and saw one of the pictures that the Arts Council had bought. It was a large canvas and I liked it for it reminded me of Vuillard. It was much more extroverted than the landscapes; even the brush strokes were more assured. It showed a woman sitting in a corner of a brightly lighted room. The browns and gold of the walls and ceiling contrasted with the faint pinkness of her dress, the grey-green newspaper left open on her lap. She stared ahead, a suggestion of a smile on her face as if she were considering the folly of the news that she had read. The impression was one of strength and stillness.

"You like that one, don't you?"

The owner of the gallery was a small, dapper man with strained and puzzled eyes and a confidential manner. He put his hand on my arm and said, "I do as well. I do. But if I were you I'd take a look at the pictures that are hanging on the wall over there. They're Anna the woman, not Anna just demonstrating her technical accomplishment. You'd make no mistake if you liked one."

He moved away before I could think of a reply. He always recommended some pictures to me and never seemed to be disappointed when I left without buying anything. I went across to the wall at the back of the second room, refusing a sherry, and saw a series of very small pictures in austere black wooden frames. At a first glance they seemed to be painted in black and white; one had to look closely to see faint touches of browns and greys. In the first picture, a woman's hand, a ring on the wedding finger, was gripping an upright rail. The knuckles and the ring were painted in detail; the rest of the hand was suggested with fast brush strokes that emphasised the tendons and a straining muscle at the wrist. Another showed the blurred dial of an alarm clock with a cigarette burning on an ashtray beside it. It was titled "Still" in the catalogue; the first was "Never". Others showed the brass rail at the bottom of a bed catching different lights as day dawned outside a window that was somewhere to the right.

"A little melodramatic," somebody said. "Insomnia is hardly a sound basis for art, is it? They're attractive but essentially superficial."

"Yes, trite," a girl's voice agreed with bored complacency. The picture that I liked most was of a Georgian window. The light from a streetlamp came in a fog of blue particles through its panes. It evoked so many mornings, waking to an empty nothingness that I decided to buy it.

"It's number twenty-two," I said to the gallery owner. "It's called 'Again'."

"I know it," he said. "It's a very nice little picture. Worth a great deal more than twenty guineas. Some of the others", he said confidentially, "in the series are rather better. But that's the one you prefer? Just wait here a minute until I put on the tag, then I'll introduce you to Anna."

I looked around curiously. The rooms were less crowded; glasses had been left on the floor. I saw a tall girl wearing a white dress talking animatedly to the Northern poet. I wrote out a cheque and when I looked up again she was standing beside me.

"Tim tells me that you've bought a picture."

"Yes, number twenty-two," I said. "The Georgian window."

"I'm glad that you like it. I hope that you still do when you take it home," she said. "Sometimes they're disappointing out of a particular context."

"I'm sure that won't happen," I said, feeling a little embarrassed that she had the duty of making polite conversation to me. "It's a very good exhibition."

"Do you really think so?"

I remember the doubt and surprise in her voice but her face is much less clear. I have to look at the photograph that appeared in the *Irish Times* on the day after she went to Belfast. Then I am reminded of a certain earnestness, a caution in the eyes, yet she is leaning forward characteristically, as if about to speak. Her hair is parted severely in the centre and she is touching the lobe of her right ear with her finger. This photograph intrigues me. It seems to be an almost perfect likeness from which a single detail has been omitted. I grope through my memory, attempting to find that detail and put it back into place but it eludes me and I see her turning away, tears shining in her eyes. It may have been the weeks filled with guilt that suppressed the reality of her image in my mind.

"I've just realised", I said, "that that's a self-portrait," pointing to the picture of the woman wearing a pink dress.

"Well, it isn't really," she said slowly. "I suppose I paint the face whose shape I know best but that's about all. Maybe it's how I'd like to be."

"You've met each other," the gallery owner said. "I'm sorry. I was trapped over there by a dreadful woman." I looked across the room and saw that Margaret was peering myopically at one of the pictures. "She reads a picture like a gossip column. Michael Waldron, Anna Lawlor," he said unnecessarily. I gave him the cheque.

"I'll get you a receipt. I'm sorry", he said to Anna, "that this vulgar trading has to go on in front of you." She laughed.

"Tim's a dear," she said to me, watching him take a stout woman by the arm to lead her unwillingly across the room. "You need a certain brashness to bring you down to earth sometimes."

"That he certainly supplies. I know your husband," I said. "I met him in Belfast just about a week ago."

"Oh, so that's why you're here," she said, without defensiveness. It was as if she had been attempting to work out a satisfactory reason for my presence there since we had met.

"Not at all," I said, "I know him only very slightly. He isn't here this evening?"

"No, it clashed with something or other which is a pity. I had hoped he could make it."

She was holding an empty sherry glass, rolling the stem between her fingers and thumb. I must not describe tensions of which I was unaware at the start, yet I remember noticing a new reserve in her manner after I had mentioned Lawlor.

"Life's rather unpredictable in Belfast," I said.

"Are you a journalist?"

"No, I was just there on a visit."

"It's a heartsick city, isn't it? I think I feel most sorry for all the children. Not only the ones who are killed but the ones who live and learn such a lot about hate. When I heard them screaming abuse and throwing stones I knew just how heartsick it was. There must be something wrong with any society that teaches kids things like that."

"Your husband would regard that as dangerously emotional."

"Yes, I suppose he would," she said. "Do you?"

47

"Not really. In the end values like that are often more sound than political objectives. A combination of both is obviously best."

"Tim's calling me," she said. "He must have made another sale. I'm delighted that you liked the show."

I had hoped to leave without being seen by Margaret but she was standing near to the door.

"Any chance of a lift?"

"Of course," I said. "I'm parked just outside."

"Well, what did you think?" she said abruptly when we were sitting in the car.

"Of the show? Very good."

"I didn't think much of it." We drove around Lincoln Place and into Merrion Square. "I don't believe that she's honest," she said. "I saw you talking to her. Do you think that she's honest?"

"I'd hardly know," I said. "It didn't occur to me to wonder. Why?"

There were hoardings outside the shell of the embassy and the park rails had been replaced. I drove past quickly as a nervous man might avoid a graveyard. The smoke from Margaret's cigarette passed in front of my eyes like a memory and I wanted to ask her something about Barbara.

"I detected all kinds of confusions," she said. "She's not honest with herself. If you want my opinion I believe that she's Lesbian but unwilling to face it. I told that dreadful little man, and he was quite annoyed."

For a ridiculous few seconds I had thought that she was speaking about Barbara.

"Oh, Anna Lawlor? What makes you think that?"

"It's in some of the paintings," she said emphatically. "An ambivalent glorification of women. There's obvious wish-fulfillment in some and then it's disguised in others. Didn't you notice?" She opened the window and threw out her cigarette. "I noticed it," she said. "And then those rather vulgar small pictures. Did you look at them?"

"I bought one of them."

"Did you? You actually liked them?"

"Not all of them," I said. "But obviously I liked the one that I bought." I felt the old hostility towards her being reawakened. "Anyway," I said, "with great respect to your psychology I think that it's complete nonsense. The differences you noticed in the paintings had nothing whatsoever to do with suppression or disguise. They're the differences that you'll find in the work of any painter whose technique is more advanced than his subject matter."

"That's a point of view," she said, and without turning I could imagine her bored expression.

"A perfectly legitimate one," I said, wondering why I cared. She lighted another cigarette.

"Oh yes," she said, "of course."

"Is Barbara back?" I asked as we turned into Wellington Road.

"Not yet," she said, after some hesitation. I wondered if she knew that we had separated, then realised that some degree of embarrassment and hurt pride lay behind my hostility. "I think it won't be for another week or two," she said.

I stopped the car and did not switch off the engine. A lorry went straining past; the thick black smoke from its exhaust remained for some seconds in a column, like a mirage.

"I was glad to see you at the gallery," Margaret said, "I wanted to have a word with you. About the other evening."

"When I called to the flat?"

"It embarrasses me," she said, and the eyes behind the thick glasses began to water. "Would you like to come in for a drink?"

I looked at my watch as if I had somewhere else to go.

"I'd like to explain," she said quickly. "I wouldn't want anyone to think that my behaviour then was typical of me."

"There's no need to explain anything. I had virtually forgotten," I said. "It's hardly any of my business."

"Yes it is in a way," she said. "You were looking for Barbara. I hate sitting in a car. Are you going to come in?"

I did not want to, but hearing something about Barbara was still irresistible. I switched off the engine and followed her to the basement door. She searched through her bag for a key.

"I've got it somewhere," she said with irritation. Her assurance was like a mood. Behind it a whole area of confidence seemed to open to defeat by the trivial. I remember watching her face as she found the key and jabbed it into the lock with unusual vehemence. Her cheeks were blotched and she was biting her lower lip like a disappointed child.

"Is whiskey all right?" she asked.

"Perfect."

"There are some clean glasses in the kitchen."

She went to get them, opening doors noisily.

"I won't be a minute," she called.

I looked around the living-room searching for traces of Barbara but could see nothing there that reminded me of her. The clock on the mantelpiece had stopped; a Pelican edition of Ernest Jones' *Life and Work of Sigmund Freud* was open on the sofa. I looked at a passage marked in pencil.

> The man who brings tears to my eyes must do a great deal before I forgive him. He is no longer my friend, and woe to him if he becomes my enemy. I am made of harder stuff than he is, and when we match each other he will find he is not my equal. As for interfering between him and Martha, 'Gnai a chi la torca', I can be ruthless!

"What's that you've got there?" Margaret said, coming in with a bottle and two glasses.

"Ernest Jones. You've marked a passage."

She put the bottle and the glasses on the table and took the book from me.

"I must have marked it ages ago," she said uneasily, putting it back on the shelf. There was a pencil beside me on the sofa. She saw me looking at it. "I'm always marking passages," she said. "I suppose it's a sloppy habit. Most of the time I can't remember why I marked them."

She was wearing a light blue blouse and dark blue linen trousers that were creased around her thighs. She poured out drinks and sat beside me on the sofa. I gave her a cigarette.

"Yes, I meant to have a word with you," she said. "About that evening."

"Do you have any water?"

"Oh, I'm sorry," she said, and the blotch marks came back, like guilt, across her face.

"Let me get it."

"No I'll get it," she said.

I went to the door of Barbara's bedroom and opened it as

silently as possible. I could hear a press being closed in the kitchen and the rattle and splash of a tap. The bedroom was even more bare than it had been; there were no clothes on the floor, no suggestion of her personality. Her acquisitiveness was almost entirely emotional.

I closed the door and was crossing the room when Margaret came back with a small jug of water. She did not seem to notice that I had moved.

"That's everything, isn't it?" she said. "I haven't forgotten anything else."

We sat down together on the sofa, side by side like an elderly couple in a church.

"Before I interrupted you," I said, "you were talking about the last time that I was here."

"Yes," she said. "I was very embarrassed afterwards. I think I might have been a little drunk."

"Aren't we all at times?"

I was suddenly very anxious to hear what she had to say. Some irrational hope that it would change everything between Barbara and myself must have prompted this interest. I am not certain why but, for a short time, I wanted that change. I wanted to suppress the unalterable truth and enjoy the escapism of believing that I had not been used in the same way as I had used her.

"I had been to a lecture," Margaret said. She drank some whiskey without adding water. "It went on later than I thought. My boyfriend was meeting me here." I attempted to picture him but failed. She would not be easy to love or even to desire. She took off her glasses and blinked as if she were exercising her eyes and I saw how easily dislike could turn to pity. "When I got back here," she said, "I found him in bed with Barbara. In my bed." I almost laughed until a stab of jealousy reminded me that she was not alone in that betrayal. I finished my whiskey and poured out more for both of us.

"So what did you do?" I asked with a curiosity that she did not seem to resent.

"What could I do? The bitch didn't care. She wasn't even disconcerted. 'Stop making a fuss,' she said. A fuss! I wish I had taken her bloody eyes out!"

We sat there in silence, both of us aware of the curious bond between us. My jealousy did not last long; this may even have been the last time that it really hurt. It was followed by relief. I had not ended something that could have lasted.

"I'm sorry," I said.

She did not reply. She stared down at her glass as if she had not heard and the knuckles of her hand were white. There were worse kinds of loneliness than mine, I thought, watching a tear come from under the rim of her glasses and move uncertainly down her cheek. I put my hand on her knee, feeling a little ridiculous, and she turned to me.

"She just didn't care and neither did he," she said with an added bitterness. "They got up and went off together. I tried to talk to him but he wouldn't sit down. 'What's happened has happened,' he said and he looked so bloody smug. I thought that he liked me."

Beneath my hand I could feel muscles tightening and loosening as if she were getting ready to spring forward.

"So they just went off," she said. "And left me here. He tried to phone me once since then but I wouldn't talk to him. I'll never forget that smug look on his face. That's why I was upset when you called."

"Who'd blame you?" I said, wondering why I was not more concerned. It is easy to look interested but more difficult to find the words that match the pretence. She looked away from me and I left my hand on her knee like a hostage.

"I'm so ashamed," she said. "I shouldn't have told you. I come so cheaply out of it all."

"Have another drink."

"Not now."

"It's always good to talk to someone," I said.

The threadbare cliché seemed to hang in the air, reproachfully, like a sigh. Another tear came down her face and caught at the corner of her mouth. She licked it away. I set down the glass and put my arm around her, regretting the meeting.

"You mustn't be upset," I said. "It's pointless now. It's better to move into the future."

She turned to me and said, "Yes, you're right. That's what I'm going to do." She closed her eyes and waited to be kissed. Her glasses bumped distractingly against my nose. I moved my hand along her thigh but felt nothing except the surprising warmth of her skin beneath the linen trousers.

"I'll take them off," she said, and I watched for a startled second until I saw that she meant her glasses. She put them carefully on the table and turned to me again like an inquisitor. I kissed her awkwardly; even without her glasses we seemed to bump ridiculously together. I put my hand on her breast, hoping that I would feel something more than embarrassment and she moved closer to me. For a minute or two, I wanted to desire her but could not. I took my hand away and my fingers, as if acting on their own initiative, began to unbutton her blouse. I remember watching them as if with surprise as they moved across the pale skin above her brassière.

"That's nice," she said, and I wondered from the way she slurred the words if she were drunk again. There were tear-stains on her face and her eyes blinked nervously. I kissed her again and said, "You're a nice girl, Margaret." She considered this ridiculous remark for a moment and said, "I'm glad you think so." I wondered what to do next. She was there in my arms, a victim of Barbara's indifference and of mine.

"Do you not mind?" she asked me.

"Mind?"

"Hearing about Barbara that night. I was afraid that you'd be hurt."

"Is that why you told me?" I said, glad of the opportunity to take my arms from around her and pour out a drink.

"Oh no," she said, "you mustn't think that. I just wanted to explain." She put her hand on my shoulder. "Should I not have told you?" she asked. "I honestly meant well."

"Did you not know we'd broken it off?"

"She never told me," she said as if this was another betrayal. "I didn't speak to her after that. She went on her holidays."

I drank some whiskey and lighted a cigarette, feeling pity and annoyance. I could see her plan for revenge, worked out so clumsily over so many bitter drinks. She would have been willing to sleep with me in an effort to hurt Barbara who would not have cared. We would have used her bed and that alone would have annoyed her. Thinking of the spartan room, the only privacy that she had, the idea appealed to me but looking at Margaret I knew that it would be a failure. She started to button her blouse but I stopped her, holding tightly on to her fingers. Fear came to her face like a blemish. She reached out to find her glasses and, ashamed, I let her go. My own desires for revenge had been no more worthy. She put on her glasses and stood up, blinking nervously at me and attempting to smile.

"You said I was nice," she said like a child who wants to hear praise being reiterated.

"You are."

"I didn't mean any harm," she said, then predictably her mood changed. She turned away and said bitterly, "I hate her." I knew that she wanted me to go. I was there like a symbol of failure confronting her with dreams that did not come true, plans left incomplete. "When he phones again," I said, "you should let him talk to you." I could hear the involuntary patronising tone in my voice.

"What would you know about it?" she said, and I knew that it was possible that she would come to hate me even more than she hated Barbara.

"You can't blame both of them equally," I said.

She sat on another chair, and crossed her legs in an effort to look relaxed.

"I don't want to talk about it," she said. "I've talked about it far too much already."

"That's fine by me."

I finished my drink and stood up to go.

"I'd better get home," I said.

"No, not yet. Please wait a minute."

The appeal in her voice suggested that she was about to concede a point at the end of a long argument. She sat up straight on the chair and said, "I value privacy. Do you?"

"Very much."

"I hate the thought of being talked about," she said. "Hate it more than anything. Can we both agree not to mention a word about all this business to anyone?"

"Of course."

She looked at me without belief and the bitterness came back to her voice.

"Neither of us came out of it very well," she said. "But she's not going to take my pride away from me."

"Who would I talk to?" I asked her. The silent clock on the mantelpiece, the empty bottles and glasses, the dusty books were like exhibits from another way of life. She stared doubtfully up at me and I imagined that I could see dislike growing darkly in her eyes.

"Very well," she said. "I think that's the best."

"I'll let myself out."

"No, I'll go," she said. She stood with me at the door and before opening it she said, without looking at me, "You think that's the best too, don't you?"

"Sure."

She opened the door; the sight of the untidy garden was like a return of reality. An empty dustbin, on which the number of the house was painted, was lying on its side. I picked it up and looked for a lid.

"No, it hasn't got one," she said. We stood there awkwardly, anxious to be apart.

"All right," she said.

"Thanks for the drinks."

"Your privacy won't be tampered with," she called, when I was at the garden gate. I could not think of an answer so I waved meaninglessly to her and got into the car. As I drove home I thought about Barbara with a return of the relief that I had felt earlier.

On my way up the stairs I met my neighbour.

"Goodnight Mr Waldron," she said. "I was hoping it was you. I was going to leave you a note."

"Is something wrong, Mrs Towers?"

"No, no," she said. "At least, I don't think so. It's just that I answered your telephone, several times. Your door was open and I felt that it might be important. It rang and rang." She brushed a strand of hair away from her eyes; she was quite excited. "The same young lady has been looking for you," she said, "from London. I've written down the details if you wouldn't mind waiting for a moment. She seemed most anxious to get you."

I stood in the doorway of her flat as she crossed the room to the old piano. I hardly knew what to think or to feel; if it were Barbara, would anything be different? I remembered Margaret's face.

"I've got it safely here for you," Mrs Towers said, taking

an envelope from the top of the piano. "A Miss Norton."

I was glad that I felt more relief than disappointment. "That's the number there," Mrs Towers said, pointing with a shaking finger at her spiky handwriting. "I hope that you can read it."

"I'm sorry that you had all this trouble, Mrs Towers."

"No trouble at all. I'm delighted to help. I don't know how important it might be. And when those girls on the ground floor are out, well, I'm alone in the house and I find the sound rather frightening. That Miss Norton," she said, "she sounded extremely pleasant. She telephoned on three separate occasions."

"She didn't leave a message?"

"Only for you to return her call. The last time I spoke to her she said it would have to be in the morning. She was going somewhere else apparently."

"Well, I'm most grateful to you for taking the message."

A cat strolled across the room and moved suspiciously around my shoes.

"I heard a discussion on the radio that's worried me," Mrs Towers said. "I wonder do you know if there's going to be a civil war?"

"Here in Ireland? I wouldn't think so."

I reread the telephone number; it was no more familiar than the name.

"I'm so glad to hear that. Some politician on the radio said that it was almost inevitable." She brushed the cat away, gently, with her foot and looked at me anxiously.

"I wouldn't worry, Mrs Towers. A lot has to go wrong yet before that happens."

I seemed to be developing an aptitude for insincere encouragement. Yet her concern made me guilty. I had not been giving sufficient thought to the tragedies around me. One can come to believe that one's own reality is the most important of all.

"Has there been some particular incident", I asked, "in the past few days that makes him think that?"

"No, I don't think so," she said. "Just the gradual deterioration. It's such a tragedy isn't it? Poor boys."

I thanked her again and went upstairs. I was certain that I did not know anyone in London called Norton. Perhaps she had used a false name, I thought, believing that I would not return the call if I knew that it was her. This did not seem likely. I tried to read some pages of my book but found them too dull. I had brought home the catalogue of Anna's exhibition; I read the biographical note. She was born in Limerick in 1945 and had attended the College of Art in Dublin. Her work had been exhibited in three group shows and in a travelling exhibition of contemporary Irish painting sponsored by the Arts Council. A number of shrewd collectors owned some of her pictures. One could hardly know less about anyone. I looked again at the London telephone number as if it contained some clue that I had been missing. When it was very dark and the room had started to grow cold, I went to bed.

Chapter Five

I dialled the London number next morning, waiting apprehensively for the sound of someone's voice. I did not know what I would say if Barbara answered. "Hold on please," a girl said, and I almost replaced the receiver. Then she said, "International Press." I could have laughed with relief, like a man who has spent a night in a haunted house and discovers, next morning, the harmless source of tappings on the wall. I asked for Miss Norton. "We're rather perturbed", she told me, "not to have received some chapters from you by now. It's the style," she added. "That's all important, you see."

"Of course."

"When will we be seeing them?"

"Very shortly," I said.

Mrs Towers was playing her piano. The tune was doleful; one pictured mourning clothes and handshakes of commiseration.

"I've been trying to reach you for some time," Miss Norton said reproachfully. "You're rather elusive. As you know, Mr Burgess expects to be visiting Dublin soon."

"Good," I said. From the flat below the notes went on with their own funereal logic towards a crescendo.

"He had hoped to be there before now but some rather more urgent jobs delayed him. However," she said, as if announcing good news, "he'll definitely be making the trip in the next few weeks."

"I look forward to meeting him."

"He'll be mainly concerned with gaining permission for the reproduction of various illustrations. But, of course, he'll want to discuss the text with you so it's vitally important that he sees some chapters soon."

"He'll certainly see them," I said. The initial relief was dissolving into irritation. "I'll send them without delay."

"I'll let him know that you promised."

"Do that, Miss Norton."

"Without any undue delay? Schedules", she said, as if repeating a dynamic company slogan, "are schedules, you know."

"Indeed they are."

"Very well then, Mr Waldron. I'll tell Mr Burgess. He'll be pleased."

I worked reluctantly for the next few days. Once, walking in Herbert Park, I saw Margaret watching some children playing with a swing. She was standing like an anxious mother, her hands in the pockets of her coat as the children screamed around her. She did not see me and I walked quickly away, relieved to have avoided a meeting. If I thought of Anna it was only because I was wondering where the picture should hang. I could find no place that seemed suitable. It demanded a plain white wall and could look incongruous, I suspected, against my landlord's damp, stained wallpaper.

The book moved forward, a tangle of crossed out paragraphs and second thoughts. Each page like each day was a small success or failure. I corrected grimly and moved on as if some escape would be found at the bottom of the last page. I was not content, yet I look back on these days with something like affection and see a stranger in an innocent world.

On the first afternoon that I did not work I went to the National Gallery to see the Armand Hammer collection. The exhibition had been open for several days. I went there to see the Vuillards and because I could think of nothing else to do.

The Vuillards disappointed me. Their tranquillity was boring; even a Paris street scene was idealised in a swirl of frozen colour that transformed vitality into a pattern that was pleasing yet oddly dull. Some other visitors to the exhibition talked loudly in a nearby room, their voices echoing along the high ceilings like a parody. "... genuine empathy ... Gauguin's sketchbook ... that ugly shoulder." I spent some time looking at Van Gogh's painting of the Hospital at Saint-Remy. There is something about melodrama that appeals to me; it catches at the mind, offering a simple remedy to emotional predicaments, like a great shout of laughter or despair. The picture was painted with all of the energy that could lie behind such a shout. Trees writhed and twisted upwards like flames to spread against a falling sky. The long, low hospital building had many of its windows shuttered, as if to prevent the mad from seeing the maniac energy of day. Before it, some stunted people walked, aimless and defeated.

"Do you like it?"

I turned and saw Anna.

"Very much," I said, "in a kind of self-interested way."

"Self-interested?"

"I see what I want to see."

"That seems sound enough."

"It's hardly a theory of aesthetics."

"Isn't it?" she said. "I'm not certain of that."

She was wearing a light brown dress. As she frowned at the picture she was not beautiful but the interest on her face was very attractive.

"I've enjoyed some of the quieter things more," she said. "Some drawings by Boudin and Pissarro. I admire this, certainly, but I can't say that I like it. Not many women would."

"Why not?"

"Oh, I'd only be guessing," she said. "Something to do with violence. As undisguised as that it isn't a part of most women's creative drive."

"Most women don't like the novels of Conrad either," I said, to fill in an awkward pause. "For some other reason."

"Why do you think that is?"

"Now you're just asking me to start guessing," I said. "Maybe it's because of the deep-rooted pessimism underneath all the irony. Or maybe it's because, despite all the belief in the forces of destiny, the men in his novels are usually more self-sufficient than women might want them to be."

"I think that Winnie Verloc is rather better than her husband."

"Up to a point," I said surprised. "But then Conrad loads the dice to make sure that you'll think so." Two elderly women looked suspiciously at a painting of two Lesbians by Von Dongen. "Grotesque," one of them said, and we did not speak again until they had gone, still muttering their disapproval.

"It's an interesting show," I said.

"Yes."

"You saw the Modigliani?"

"Yes, I liked it."

"Isn't it extraordinary", I said, forcing on the conversation as I had forced on sentences and paragraphs, "how often he distorted faces in the very same way, the same elongation, and yet the character exposed in the faces is always different. Somehow or other he avoided parody."

"Yes, but his people are very self-contained," she said. "Can you imagine any one of them existing outside the moment of the picture? It's a beautifully introspective world that makes so many others seem unreal."

I discovered, much later, that the conversation had been just as forced and difficult for her as for me. She liked to go to galleries alone and hated any talk about pictures. She had spoken to me only because she suspected that I had seen her. "I really was tempted", she told me in Amsterdam, "to tiptoe into another room. I hated having to make solemn remarks to sound judicious. It stopped me feeling anything at all about the pictures."

I asked her if she would come for a drink. She hesitated and looked at her watch and then, as if unable to think of a credible excuse, agreed. "But not a drink," she said. "A cup of tea. I might do some work later."

We drove to Dawson Street forcing disconnected remarks on each other like people practising a new language. I found parking space outside the Mansion House.

"I've never learned to drive," she said as we went up the steps of the Hibernian Hotel. "Isn't that stupid? I know that it's something that everyone should be able to do."

The lounge was full of Americans. They called to each other

across the glass-topped tables and noisily counted their change. A very old woman with startling blue hair said "Waiter! Waiter!" and then lapsed into silence, slumped, like a doll, on her chair as if the effort had been too great. We found a table near to the dining-room door and ordered afternoon tea.

"So you *are* interested in pictures," Anna said, as if conceding a point.

"Why do you say that?"

"Whenever a friend of Peter's comes to a show, I assume they've been press-ganged into it."

"Really? And if they buy a picture?"

"Then I'm really suspicious," she said.

"I'm not actually a friend of his," I said. "I've just met him here and there a couple of times."

"In Belfast?"

"Yes. The last time."

"Do you think that he's safe there?"

"I'm sure that he is."

"It's a worry," she said. "It's probably not at all so bad if you're there. There must be ways of avoiding danger." A clock on a mantelpiece chimed, a thin, nervous tinkle, and she crumbled a piece of sandwich on her plate. "But thinking about it from a distance I imagine that every day he's having narrow escapes."

"It's much less dramatic than that."

"You think so?"

"Especially when you can choose where to live."

"I know that I told you about the children," she said. "I thought that was really terrible."

"Does he enjoy reporting from there?" I asked her, feeling a sudden curiosity about the nature of their relationship.

"Yes, I suppose that he does," she said. "It's a chance to make a name for himself. It's an ill wind," she added with what might have been bitterness but she smiled as she said it. "His by-lines are on the front page most days."

"He's a good reporter," I said for some reason that I cannot recall. She looked at me for a moment as if she had suspected my dishonesty. "Yes, he is," she said. "I'm sure of that."

"Did he get down yet for the exhibition?"

"No."

I waited for her to give some conventional explanation and felt embarrassment pass like a chill between us when she did not say anything else.

"That's very bad luck," I said. "I suppose that it's the price of by-lines."

"The show lasts for another week. He's coming down here next weekend. Did you really like that picture you bought?" she asked me unexpectedly.

"Very much indeed."

She poured out more tea for both of us and the action, like the question, seemed to be a device for changing the conversation. The old American woman walked with unpredictable agility across the lounge. She was carrying a large black bag and a number of magazines.

"Our disappearing tourist industry," I said, watching the blue head vanish through an arch towards the telephone boxes. We reverted to forced conversation that lumbered awkwardly on as an alternative to silence. I have forgotten most of what was said but, soon before we left, I remember her asking me if I had ever been to Amsterdam.

"Once," I said. "A couple of years ago."

"I'm hoping to go there soon."

"It's a very beautiful city. The nicest I've ever seen."

"Is it?" she asked with all the anxious eagerness of someone who wants to hear a compliment being repeated. When I try to decide if I loved her, this is one of the moments that I recall. It is often impossible to explain why certain pieces of trivia can come together to form an emotion. Accidental words may create a moment more deeply sensual than any experienced while making love. There is no logic in this progression of feeling, no slow awakening of interest leading on to natural tenderness or passion or dislike.

"Incredibly beautiful," I said. "And perfectly preserved. I keep meaning to go back."

I remember the way that interest brightened on her face as if I had offered her a key and a marked map for an escape plan. I felt no passion or lust but something more than curiosity made me look at her carefully and remember. It is certainly true that I was lonely and more than usually vulnerable to self-deception. I was like a hermit who must go on believing fanatically in a God to keep himself sane. I am reluctant to believe that she was simply an alternative to Barbara, as a truly religious man would be unwilling to accept that God is merely an alternative to despair. It debased us both; yet at the start this is probably what she was. Our interest in others is far too often a disguised interest in ourselves; we use them like pieces on a board to plan out our own winning moves, our own small triumphs. I was disappointed, and although the jealousy no longer hurt it was there like defeat. If forced to explain my feelings, I would have said that I had been cheated. I have sometimes felt like a character trapped forever in a role in some bad farce. I move from room to room through a baffling succession of doors as others bang shut, always missing, by seconds, the reality that a confrontation would bring. No amount of planning, however successful, can rid me entirely of the thought that if I had opened a door some seconds earlier or waited behind a curtain I might have discovered a meaning in the meaningless events.

I looked at her across the table; she was fiddling with a key. Around us the nasal American voices went on in a tone of perpetual complaint. It is important for me to understand my motives and to make her real. No farce could adequately encompass the tragic inanity of the events that were to follow if we had not at least got some real interest in each other, some movement towards love. I believe that she liked me at first and that is some consolation. It helped to kill guilt. I know that I decided at an early stage that I would not use her and that I would not risk being used. I had learned both of these lessons with Barbara. If I had not done so the events would have been different or would not have happened. That is the farce; the pieces of an old, dead life that we carry with us like confusion into the new. We infect others with our past; they breathe it in without knowing, take it in our words and kisses and silences.

"I'm going to go there", she said, "when the show is over. I want to see the Vermeers."

"Is Peter interested in painting?"

"Not really," she said. "But he's not uninterested either. He likes some things." She put the key in her pocket. "I think he dislikes all the space that I take up," she said. "All the rags and boxes and pieces of board and newspapers spread on the floor. It's very intrusive in a small flat. All that he needs is a typewriter." She smiled. "That's bound to colour his attitude," she said. "Maybe that's why he likes Belfast."

I remember looking for a critical undertone in her words but being unable to find it. She smiled across at me, polite and disengaged. We might have been discussing the weather.

"Have you been married for long?" I asked her. "I don't remember hearing."

"For nearly two years now," she said. "Two years next October. It seems much shorter than that."

"Before you go to Amsterdam, I must lend you a book," I said. "It's particularly good."

"About the galleries?"

"Yes, and the rest of the city. It follows each canal."

"I'd love to read it."

"Good. I'll get it to you."

"I'm afraid that I'd better go. I've got some work," she said, looking vaguely around the crowded lounge as if expecting to be reminded of the nature of the task by something that she would see there.

"Let me give you a lift."

"Please don't bother," she said. "I've only got to go to Pembroke Street. I'll be there in five minutes."

"Are you sure?"

"I'd like the walk."

I watched her leave the lounge and my interest followed her. I found myself speculating on her movements, guessing at her thoughts. I would have liked to be with her in her room, sitting, watching her painting; the boxes, the rags, the boards, the newspapers spread across the floor. For some reason that I cannot remember now or even start to imagine, this image seemed to hold out promises of safety and peace.

I went down the street to Brown and Nolan's bookshop and looked through their travel section. I could find no book on Amsterdam that matched the description of the one that I had claimed to own but I selected a large, illustrated history of the city. The photographs reminded me of my stay there in a way that made me envy her; the calm, civilised canals, the trams swinging around corners. I looked at them that night before I went to bed and wanted to be with her when she walked along

Kalverstraat, hearing the music of a barrel-organ or sitting outside a café in the Spui or going up the narrow stairs behind the bookcase to the room where Anne Frank lived.

I waited for a week with the patient, jungle cunning of the wounded animal. I wanted, each day, to telephone her and arrange to deliver the book but Barbara had made me wary. I would make no mistakes; it was going to be honest this time and unrushed and, hopefully, real. On the Monday after the exhibition of her paintings closed, I went to the gallery. The work of some other artist was being put on the walls; her pictures were stacked in a passage and when I looked again at the one that I had bought it was smaller and less evocative than I had remembered.

"Very nice," the gallery owner said to me, his eyes shifting into the room where a small fat man with a beard was giving directions on the hanging of his pictures. "That's a very nice picture. You've made no mistake." He put his hand on my arm as if about to impart a confidence. "They sold very well," he said. "She's a good girl. Are you coming to the opening on Wednesday?"

"I don't think I'll be able to make it," I said. The pictures that I could see were like enlarged impressions of ceramic tiles. "And to be honest I don't really find them interesting."

"They're to cover the walls in businessmen's offices," he said, guiding me down the passage, his hand on my shoulder. "They go with tubular steel furniture. But who am I to raise my voice against them? If he weren't such a pompous ass I'd even forgive him his lack of talent. He paints with a compass," he said when we reached the door of his office. "Miss What in here will wrap up your picture for you."

A small, grey-haired woman put sheets of corrugated paper around the picture and tied it as elaborately as if she were gift-wrapping a purchase in a store at Christmas. He watched her with an air of surprise. "That's very nice, Miss What." She ignored him and tied another knot, one end of the string held firmly between her teeth.

"Some people like them," he said to me. "They're easy to live with, you see. You'd never have your values threatened by three parallelograms and a rhombus."

"I'm glad her exhibition did well," I said.

"Anna? She deserves it. She works hard."

"Did her husband manage to get here?"

"No," he said, looking at me with what may have been suspicion. "You know him?"

"Not well."

"Nor do I. Do you like him?"

"I've just met him once or twice," I said. "She mentioned to me that he hoped to get down before the end of the week."

"Yes, she mentioned that to me as well. Something must have prevented it. Miss What has done a very neat job," he said. "You didn't know Anna before?"

"Not before meeting her here."

"She's rather special," he said. "I must confess that she makes me feel a little paternal."

The small woman left the room, banging the door behind her.

"I used to think that it was the difficult age," he said, "but it's gone on for far too long. Fifteen years of bad temper. But she keeps the books neatly. Anyway, as I was saying, I feel mildly paternalistic towards Anna. She needs a lot of encouragement and minding. Did you get that impression?"

"You forget I hardly know her," I said, irritated by his questions. They seemed to infer that I was doing some damage to her.

"Forgive me," he said. "All this rush, all this fuss with that ass out there is bad for me. I'd better get back. I'm glad that you got such a good picture." We went up the passage and the bearded artist said, "The lighting. My God! Those lights! It's like a setting for a gynaecological operation. They've got to be changed."

"You worry far too much. Those lights are particularly perfect."

"Well, if nobody else cares a damn..."

I went out to the car and my irritation lasted for most of the journey home. When I got there I dialled her number but there was no reply. A letter had arrived from Burgess. "I have at last received the three chapters," he wrote, "and will let you have my opinion of them in due course. Please continue towards completion of the text in the meantime so that there will be no more unnecessary delay. When sending you my comments I will let you know the date of my arrival in Dublin." A chilliness punctuated the words. I could imagine Miss Norton typing them.

I tried Anna's number again and listened to the ringing tone for long after I knew that it would not be answered. It was cold in the room; there were cobwebs in the corners and hanging from the ceiling. The next time that I dialled the number it was answered; for several seconds I hardly knew what to say.

"I wanted to lend you that book."

"That's nice. I thought that you'd forget."

I would not have known her voice. "I don't mean that I assumed it specifically about you," she said. "It's just that most people do."

"Do you know when you're going yet?"

"Not yet. I haven't had a chance to plan it. But soon. It has to be before the schools open", she said, "and I start classes."

"Would you care to have a drink?"

In the pause before she answered I could hear the ghost of a voice saying "Is that Mullingar? Is that Mullingar?"

"If that's not inconvenient," she said.

"Not at all. I'd like it. I'll bring the book. Where's the best place to meet?"

"How about the Hibernian?" she said. "I'm not very fond of the pubs around here."

"That's perfect. In about an hour?"

It was an awkward meeting. I remember the silences more clearly than the conversation. We made each other defensive with our wariness, exchanging remarks as if they were concessions in negotiation. I was drinking whiskey and must have been nervous for I remember speaking too loudly and being emphatic about something on which I held no real opinion. I told her that I had collected the picture but could not decide on the place where it should hang.

"Probably a bedroom," she said. "It's an early morning picture."

She was flicking through the pages of the book, pausing to look with interest at some of the illustrations.

"I was hoping you'd help me," I said without much hope.

"Help you?"

"To choose a spot."

"All right," she said, so unexpectedly that I almost laughed with pleasure.

"I suppose", she said, "that it's vanity but I'm often curious to see what they look like when they're hanging somewhere else. There's one in the reception hall of an Insurance Company in Baggot Street. The light's all wrong and it looks like something done by a retarded child as occupational therapy. I'm sometimes tempted to go in and try to steal it."

"Let me know if you need a hand," I said.

"I just might take you up on that!"

Our laughter was like the end of a sexual tension. She blushed and finished her drink.

"Could you come over now?" I asked.

"All right."

"There's no reason to believe", she said in the car, "that I'll be any better than you are at choosing a place."

"You're certain to be."

"It doesn't follow."

"Well, it's worth finding out," I said. "You'll know about the light anyway. Have you seen the pictures for the new exhibition at the Nassau?"

"Brian's new work? A few of them. They're interesting, aren't they?"

"Not to me."

She sat very still beside me, the Amsterdam book open on her knees. She was wearing blue denim jeans and a heavy jacket that had paint smudges on one sleeve.

"He's trying for something," she said.

I wondered if we would make love. I had become so concerned with caution that I knew that there was a possibility that we would not even kiss. My instincts were not acquisitive. I did not want her in the careless, impersonal way that one might want some girl picked up at a party. All of my planning had been more concerned with avoiding loneliness or jealousy than anything more positive. I remember a reflection of her face in the driving mirror as we turned into Raglan Road.

"He didn't come down," she said, abruptly, as if ending a conversation.

"Your husband?"

"Yes."

"That's bad luck."

"Yes," she said, "it is."

"He must be very busy."

"I suppose so," she said. I parked the car. "You know those Renaissance paintings", she said, "where buildings or something in the background are just as sharp and clear as figures in the foreground? It's a quite impossible thing. The eye can't see that way. But that's the way that I've started to think about him now. My eyes can't detach him from Belfast and all those terrible streets and ruins and spots where people died."

"You should get him to come back to Dublin," I said with an unease that came like desire. I remembered Margaret's sad attempt at revenge and my own resentment towards Barbara. I felt ashamed of the selfishness of my reaction but caution was too deeply ingrained. I knew that if I had to choose again between loneliness and jealousy, I would decide to be alone.

She climbed the steps before me and stood like a hostess at the door. "I used to know someone who lived a few doors away," she said. "It's a nice road." As we went up the stairs the banisters creaked beneath her hand and I was more aware than usual of the cobwebs that hung like commemorative banners from the ceiling and of the dust on the landing window.

"You mustn't suffer from vertigo," she said when we reached my flat. She was making conversation with a confidence that I did not feel. "I like that Souter," she said, looking at one of the three pictures that I owned.

While I made coffee I could hear her taking books from the shelves. "A collected Conrad!" she called as if she had discovered books that betrayed some surprising or esoteric interest.

"Borrow some of them if you like."

"And spoil your theory?"

When I went back to the living room she was sitting in an armchair, flicking through *Under Western Eyes*.

"I haven't read this," she said, "but I must admit that it looks a bit indigestible. Should I accept a challenge?"

We talked for a while in the casual, desultory manner of a married couple in a rut. Perhaps it was her ring that reminded me or something about the way that she collected my cup and took it back to the kitchen. She had taken off her jacket and I noticed the shape of her body with some of the old acquisitiveness. I was curious about her and with it came some resentment at how little I knew.

"Have you painted much recently?" I asked her.

"Not much. I've been sketching a little," she said. "The thought of an exhibition is a kind of crutch. It helps the work along. It's not so easy to get down to when there isn't some pressure. Would you like me to look at the walls?"

We went into the bedroom. I had left the painting on the mantelpiece. She said, "I'm a little embarrassed," walking over to it. "It's a little like meeting someone you used to know when you were young and having nothing to say to them. You know the way that you grow away from people. It's always sad and embarrassing. You'd like to be able to remember something that matters but all that comes back is a face or a name."

"I've sometimes forgotten both. Only the other day," I said, "I had a conversation with someone whom I'd have sworn I never knew, but he kept on remembering the nicknames of teachers and things that had happened at rugby matches."

"Over there," she said, pointing to a spot on the wall opposite to the window. "That's the place."

"But the wallpaper . . ."

"Isn't exactly ideal," she said. "But it's the proper place. You'll see it when you wake up."

There were ink-stains on the cover of the bed. I had no idea of how they had got there or why I had not noticed them before.

"I'll get a hook in the morning," I said. She was looking out of the window. "This must be a perfect view in autumn," she said. "I always liked those trees. And that church. Do they still walk in procession on Sundays?"

"Yes, I think so."

As she came back across the room I put my hands on her arms. She looked at me, puzzled, for a moment, as if I had claimed acquaintanceship on the street.

"Was this the whole point?" she asked.

"Not at all. I wanted to know . . ."

"Not all of it anyway?"

"No."

"As a variation on etchings?"

"Not at all. But now that you're here . . ."

"What?" she asked without hostility, and I kissed her.

She moved a little closer to me but showed no other response, and when we moved apart I was almost reluctant to look at her. I sat on the edge of the bed and it creaked as if we were in some cheap brothel. I held out my hand. She took it and sat beside me like a friend.

"Did you *want* to kiss me," she asked, "or was it just the conventional thing to do?"

"I wanted to."

"Why?"

"Why not?" I said inadequately, unable to hide my irritation. A pigeon moaned down the chimney and children's voices came faintly from the garden.

"I just wondered if you thought that I expected it."

"No," I said, and my fingers moved across her wedding ring. "I've never been able to be introspective about desire. Or I've never wanted to be."

"That's probably right," she said. I kissed her again, feeling like a housebreaker who is caught when the lights go on and the door opens. She kept her lips tightly closed so that even when we lay back on the bed it was like a charade, an empty ritual amongst the ink-stains. She took my hand away from her breast and looked up at me, and I saw to my surprise that she was frightened. I sat up and said, "I'm sorry."

"No, don't be," she said. "It's got nothing to do with you. But I can't help being introspective. It's the implications that frighten me."

"Need there be implications?"

"Surely there have to be?"

"But not outside your control."

"I don't know," she said. "Maybe it's faith that I lack. The faith to be spontaneous. Or to believe in anyone else's spontaneity. Does that make sense?"

"Of a sort."

"What a dreadful bore for you," she said. "I know. It's even boring for me." She sat beside me and I felt bitterness twist through my mind like a rage. It was far too strong to have been provoked by her and I tried to hide it but must have failed. She put her hand on mine and said, "I'm sorry."

"You shouldn't be," I said.

"Yes of course I should. It's not fair to subject someone to a range of reflex actions that they didn't cause."

"We do it all the time," I said.

"That doesn't make it any more fair. If I could believe, simply, that you wanted me, simply, that would make me quite happy."

"Would it?"

"I'm afraid that it would."

"You're afraid?" I said, to gain some time.

"That's just an expression," she said.

I could feel involvement closing in around me like a fog bringing blindness with it. "Is there any difference between a desire for simple happiness and a lack of courage?" I asked. "We're not all that different. You don't want to be used. Neither do I."

"In what sense?"

"Turned into a fantasy or used as an object. Depersonalised," I said, wondering if it were ever possible. Perhaps what we call spontaneity is as preordained as fate, as if our emotions respond to some genetic factor. I felt hypocritical as I sat beside her on the bed, her fingers moving slowly across the back of my hand in what would have been a sign of affection if we had been much older. There had been nothing spontaneous about my actions. I had planned as coldly as Barbara. Her leg was pressing close against mine; something like a memory of lust loomed in through the fog and the moaning went on in the chimney.

"It's being married," she said. "It naturally makes things more complicated."

"Of course."

"I might as well admit that I wasn't ever very relaxed, but marriage makes it worse."

"Does it?" I asked, looking at her face as if I could find some line or shadow there that would confirm the truth of her words. The lips that I had kissed moved involuntarily, like nerves, and she looked away from me. Her marriage had left no obvious bitterness on her face; perhaps there had not been time. I had seen it happen too often to girls whom I had known or to the wives of friends; the lines of disappointment and irony as passion died amongst the prams, the worry about bills and the old routine. I reached out and touched her cheek. Its coldness against my fingers was almost shocking.

"If you are afraid," I said, "I've done nothing much to reassure you."

She looked at me gratefully.

"But how can I show that I want you, simply, except by making love?"

"That could show so many other things that might have nothing at all to do with me."

"No."

"Yes it can."

"No, Anna," I said, suddenly aware of my own voice. It sounded as if I were correcting a disobedient child. "If you've got faith in yourself . . ."

"I believe in myself," she said, "that's a different thing. I know what I am. That requires no assent to mysteries. You can believe strongly in yourself and still be afraid of discovering something that would destroy everything else."

"That's far too vague."

"It's meant to be," she said. "Why should I have to sit here and explain?"

"You don't have to," I said as she stood up angrily. "There are a dozen pleasant ways of saying no. Believe me, I've heard every one of them. So if you're in love with your husband or whatever other reason, that's all right by me. But I won't apologise for wanting you."

"I'd hate you to do that," she said.

"Why?"

"Because I'd like to believe that it's true."

"Have you ever had the feeling", I asked her, "that you're right back where you started?"

She smiled and said, "I know."

"You're beautiful," I said insincerely or perhaps from some curiosity to see her reaction.

"Do you think so?" she said. "I don't. The two halves of my face don't really add up. When I try a self-portrait I'm always tempted to put two left sides together." She pressed at her face with her fingers as if she were moulding clay.

"How well do you know Peter?" she asked me.

"I'm sure that I've told you before. Not very well. Just well enough to say hello to when we meet or to go for a drink."

"He's never talked about me?"

"Nothing much. That you painted. I didn't even know that he was married until we met in Belfast."

"I'm often curious about how other people see him," she said. "I suspect that he's quite different when I'm not there but, of course, I've no way of knowing."

"Do you think he sleeps around in Belfast?" I asked treacherously.

A blush moved slowly across her face as if she had heard some unexpected criticism. I wanted to reach out and offer her affection, believing that I had found a clue to the complex evasion of her words. She stared at me and I felt both uneasy and ashamed.

"No, I wouldn't think so," she said. "Why do you ask?"

"Just one or two things that you said."

"Are you telling me that he does?"

"I haven't the faintest idea," I said, watching the colour fade away from her face. "It was a singularly boorish thing to say. Hell hath no fury like a man who doesn't know why he's been scorned."

"No, I'm sure that he doesn't," she said, as if she had not heared me. "He's not like that."

"Good," I said with some bitterness. "Would you like a drink? I've got a little whiskey next door."

"All right."

"I'm sorry", I said, when we were sitting in the living-room, "for being so bloody clumsy."

"Well, it was the bedroom," she said with a surprising frankness that I did not know how to interpret. "I'd hardly have been there, would I, if I wasn't expecting something to happen?"

"Would you not?"

"I assumed that after we looked at the picture . . . I just hoped that you wanted to know about hanging it as well."

"I don't understand," I said.

"How could you?"

"Are you happily married?"

"I don't actually know," she said after some consideration. "Not knowing what anyone else feels, I can't really say if what I feel is happiness or not. I certainly love Peter if that's what you mean."

"Not really."

"It isn't enough? That's what I feel as well. Sometimes. There are problems", she said, revolving the whiskey glass slowly between her fingers, "that make it difficult enough to define happiness. Sometimes I'm very happy."

"What kind of times?"

"It must be your turn by now to admit something about yourself."

"I'm not very good at it," I said. "I've got into the habit of telling people what they want to hear. It makes for a quieter sort of life."

"Is that what you've been doing with me?"

"No, something went wrong," I said, "which convinces me that my usual practice is by far the wisest."

I felt like someone betrayed, surrounded by old, lost hopes and new disappointments. I could hear the sounds that the pigeons made on the roof; their claws were scrabbling against the slates as if they were attempting, desperately, to save themselves from falling. It was getting cold in the room and she looked at her watch, an action that I could have predicted. I have never been good at avoiding moments of self-pity.

"I suppose that I'd better go," she said.

"I'll take you home."

"Do you mind?"

"I'd like to."

We drove to Pembroke Street.

"I'll give you back your book", she said, "as soon as I've read it."

"Keep it for as long as you like."

"I'm sorry about all the vagueness," she said as we stopped near to the Pembroke Bar. "I know that I just gave mysterious kinds of answers to the questions that you asked me."

"It's none of my business," I said. "I'm sorry that you felt cross-questioned."

"No, confused," she said. "But not by the questions. I'm beginning to feel disloyal and I don't know whether that's something to be ashamed of or if I should be glad. I don't really know the rules."

"In most of the things that matter there aren't any rules."

A bus stopped behind us, its brakes squealing like a wounded animal, and an old beggar woman came down the path, pushing an empty pram towards her usual place outside Gaj's Restaurant.

"I'd like to see you again," I said, "if that's all right with you."

"Would you really?" She seemed to be genuinely surprised.

"Of course."

"I'd have thought that you'd cut your losses."

"Whatever you might feel disloyal to," I said, "don't let it make you cynical."

"Perhaps I'm just self-important. Disloyalty is rather a large concept."

She was looking out of the side window of the car. I could see her cheek and, just above the collar of her jacket, a nerve that tightened and relaxed like a fist. She turned around slowly. "I'd like to see you," she said. She reached out and took my hand, and as the cars went past we kissed uncomfortably, the steering wheel pressing against my ribs. Her tongue tasted faintly of whiskey. Whenever I walk down Pembroke Street now, I remember that taste and the feel of her breasts beneath my fingers and the way that she cried. There were tears on her face and her shoulders jerked but she made no sound, as if she were miming a parody of grief. When I attempted to comfort her, she pressed back against the door and tried to say something, shaping a silent word with her lips.

"I wish you'd tell me what it is," I said, inadequately, attempting to take her hand. "I'm obviously making things worse for you. I don't want to do that."

"I know," she said with difficulty. I gave her a handkerchief and she wiped her face, looking into the driving mirror. "Oh God," she said, "whenever I have a nightmare it's about being hysterical in public. Only a few nights ago I dreamed that I was sitting in a cinema with someone, maybe Peter. Then, for no reason that I could understand, I started to scream. I went on and on and all the people were staring at me or started to move away. And whoever I was with said, 'Shut up. You're making a fool of us.' But I couldn't stop. I tried to but the screaming went on as if it were coming from someone else. Even the people on the screen stopped acting and stared at me. Peter tells me that I'm too self-absorbed. He's almost certainly right."

"In my experience," I said, "whenever someone tells you that you're self-absorbed it simply means that they don't like what you're thinking."

My treachery was now without caution. I regretted the time spent waiting and planning ahead, crouched in my caution like an animal in a wood. I wanted to wound Lawlor, to attack from behind, to restore my own self-esteem as if it were he who had damaged it. I was moving in, like Margaret, for revenge although her plan had at least some logic. She had not picked blindly on strangers when she planned to bare her body and use it like a knife.

"Are you sure that he loves you?" I asked her, in an attempt to draw some blood.

"How can anyone be sure that they're loved?"

There was no need to plant doubt. It was flourishing somewhere in her mind like a poison plant. I could see it in her eyes and I am ashamed to remember my irrational feeling of victory, as if I could force her to love me by destroying her world. I was there like a false prophet with specious promises of salvation for anyone who would help pull down idols and smash altars.

"One can sometimes tell," I said and for some moments I feared that my duplicity would be as obvious as her doubt.

"Have you ever been sure?"

"I've known the opposite," I said, unable to make so impossible a claim. "I've known when I wasn't loved."

"For me it's like an anagram. The longer that I stare at it the more words I can see. Not all of them please me." She smiled, blinking the last trace of tears from her eyes and said, "That's probably the self-absorption. Trying to find the forty-seventh word."

If I had not been so hurt, I would not have been so intent on hurting. I even like to believe that if she had been happily married I would have acted differently. This is not an account of love but of failure and farce; I cannot justify myself. I can only attempt to explain why I acted as I did. My jealousy had gone underground, but remained there, treacherous as a marsh. I had been marked by Barbara's indifference more deeply than I could ever have been marked by her love. I was scarcely aware of this until later yet when I said, "That doesn't sound very good," I knew that the blow was directed at somebody else.

Another bus squealed behind us as Anna opened the book on Amsterdam.

"This is hope," she said. "I believe in somewhere else. Do you think that's the origin of Heaven?" Her fingers moved across a picture of the Rijksmuseum as if by touching, like Thomas, she could have some old belief confirmed. "I know I'm overtired," she said hopelessly, and I wanted to touch her, to feel her breasts again and believe in my own salvation. "Are you sure that you like your picture?"

"Very much," I said. "I like it more each time that I see it."

"I remember painting it," she said. "Do you mind my saying that I did it with some contempt, not for it but for myself?"

"That doesn't change it."

"Doesn't it? I think that it probably does but I don't know how. It was like giving way to self-pity," she said, unaware of how well I could understand. "So it must be a simplification, like my sitting here and crying, and your pretending interest."

"What pretence?" I asked her but when my arms were around her I knew that desire had been driven away by talk. Her body was warm. I kneaded her skin beneath my fingers like a potter and hoped that she would not notice the difference. I knew that if we had gone into her flat to make love it would have been a failure, violence opening between us like a wound.

"Oh God," she said suddenly, "anyone could recognise us! So near to my door." She looked out of the windows as if expecting to see accusing fingers. Two girls in brown school uniforms looked scornfully into the car as they went past. We must have looked old to them and rather pathetic.

"Such a stupid thing to do," Anna said. I saw that she was trembling.

"No one would have noticed."

"They could have."

A note of panic came like passion into her voice. "So stupid!" she said again as she bent to look up at the windows of the houses opposite. "I'd better go in."

"When will I see you again?"

"Not for a while," she said.

"Why not?"

"Please. I know that it's boring, but please. A week?" she said as if making an offer for some item on a stall. "Just to give me a chance . . ." The unfinished sentence lay heavily between us like some new understanding. "I'm sorry," she said, "I know that it's complicated."

"In a week then. I'll be looking forward to seeing you."

I watched her walk away and go into a house. She did not look back. I should have felt a need for some caution then but a selfish belief in the future had covered my unease. When I attempted, in the days ahead, to analyse her behaviour I always stopped before arriving at a conclusion that might disconcert. I should have gone through the inconsistencies, like a maze, to the heart of the confusion but I remained outside, allowing only safe speculation. I wondered how I would put down the week. The thought of meeting her lay before me like a challenge; the time in between was a compound of boredom and excitement. On one of the days, I decided that I would visit Belfast again.

Chapter Six

At first, I was not sure that I was being followed. I had seen him on the Falls Road, staring across at me as if he were trying to remember my name. He was wearing an old blue raincoat. Women with shopping bags pushed past him and he moved back into a doorway as if taking shelter from rain. A woman grabbed me by the arm and said, "All the same. All the bloody same." She was drunk; the crumpled face looked up at me like the face of an accident victim and tears began to seep from her eyes. "What the hell did you ever do?" she asked me but before I had to reply she had pounced on someone else. "And what about you? Were you there or weren't you? Tell me that."

When I looked again, he had gone. I felt no relief. He had prompted curiosity, not fear. Ten minutes later, walking down a narrow street, I stopped to look at a burnt-out house and saw him. He was standing about twenty yards away, lighting a cigarette. I felt some apprehension. I did not even know what part of the city I was in. I had left the Falls Road and gone past rows of terrace houses and burnt-out sites. I remember looking around for a clue, some poster or hoarding or piece of bunting that would reveal the politics of the street, but there was nothing.

I walked on quickly, anxious to see if he would follow. I turned into another street, hearing his footsteps behind me like a mocking echo. He was not attempting to hide. When I glanced back I saw him walking in the middle of the street, his hands in the pockets of his coat. I was going to stop and wait for him but did not and when he continued to follow I gave up hope that it might be coincidence. I knew that if I knocked at the doors of any of the houses I would not be admitted. In these streets a knock at the door, like a strange face at the window or the sound of running feet, could be murder.

I tried to work out what turns would bring me back towards the centre of the city. It had started to rain; a pigeon scrabbled at something in the gutter until a dog moved towards it, slinking along the pavement like a shadow. I believed that if I took several left turns I would find my way back towards a place that I would recognise. On the gable ahead I could read the word *Bernie* but the rest of the message had been obliterated. I turned into another street. Some children were playing nearby. "We're the IRA now," one of them was shouting. "We're the IRA. Ye're the soldiers." It was a slender clue but enough to assure me for a moment that I was still on Republican streets. A dustbin lid clattered to the ground and when its echoes died away I realised that I could no longer hear footsteps. I went back to the corner and looked but the street was empty. "You can't do that," an unseen child screamed. "When you're dead you have to stay on the ground." I lighted a cigarette and could have laughed with the relief that I felt. The streets of the city could pull at one's nerves like despair.

I decided to take the turns that I had planned. I walked up the street, and the man stepped out from the corner of an intersecting lane. Another man wearing a dark brown anorak joined him. "Walk slowly towards us," he said. "There's someone behind you." He held his arm out stiffly as if pointing into the distance; it was only then that I saw the revolver in his hand. "Come on!" he said as I hesitated, and the man in the blue raincoat took a step towards me.

When I reached them, he searched me, pushing roughly at my pockets and slapping along my legs.

"Nothing," he said with what might have been disappointment.

"What is this?" I asked.

Someone behind me laughed. I turned and saw a boy who could not have been more than fifteen. His youth was more disconcerting than the iron bar that he carried. "You'll soon find out," he said.

"That's enough," the man in the anorak said. He put the revolver into his pocket. "You'll take a walk with us," he said to me, "and if you know what's good for you, you'll do what you're told. Now walk." He had worried, bloodshot eyes and shaving cuts on his chin.

"I don't know who you think I am," I said as I walked between them down the street.

"It isn't what we think. Now shut up."

A woman came out of the door of a house. When she saw us, she hesitated, then turned and went back inside. The door banged loudly and a child began to wail.

"Can I ask who you are?"

"You can't. And you talk too bloody much."

The man in the raincoat sniggered sycophantically, then cleared his throat and spat. He sniggered again like the stooge in a comedy duo and said, "That's telling him." I remember thinking that death would be utterly incongruous with that sound in one's ears. We went down a lane.

"In here."

The house was deserted and most of its windows were broken. There was cracked, brown linoleum on the kitchen floor; a pile of rubbish had been swept into one corner.

"Get up the stairs."

We entered what must once have been the bedroom of a teenage girl. There was no furniture but some coloured pictures from fan magazines were taped around the walls. The pop groups were posed provocatively, guitars held like weapons, bestriding a fantasy world. There was glass in the window. I looked down into a small backyard where litter had accumulated as if it were used as a dump.

"All right," the man in the anorak said. "Who are you?"

"Why the hell should I tell you that?" I asked with sudden, unwise annoyance. I heard a snigger from behind me, then I was hit on the back of the neck. The blow was more surprising than painful, but I staggered forward.

"You'll tell me," he said, taking out the revolver and snapping off the safety catch. It looked heavy and old-fashioned. I thought that I could see a trace of rust on the barrel. "If you value your knee-caps you won't waste my time."

"Do you want me?" the boy who had stayed downstairs called up hopefully.

"I told you to stay where you are. Now empty your pockets, you."

He gave the revolver to the man behind me and looked at the letter from Burgess. I tried to remember if there was any possible ambiguity in its tone. I had jotted some notes on the envelope. He read them out slowly and with difficulty, his lips moving, "Davitt's attitude to the O'Shea affair . . . Tim Healey . . . the clerical influence." He made this sound like a message in code. His worried eyes looked at me as if he had discovered all that he wanted to know. As he started to read the letter, I wondered if he belonged to either branch of the IRA. If he did, the fact that I came from Dublin would not, in itself, be a sign of some obscure guilt. If he were a Loyalist or one of the plain-clothes members of the British Army who were known to work in Belfast, then the situation might be even more difficult. I watched him, fear growing like a memory, and with it a strong resentment that he could hold such power.

"So you come from Dublin?" he said as he folded the letter and put it into his pocket. "What's all this stuff about Davitt?"

"It's for a book."

The man behind me sniggered.

"Do you know the Burlington Hotel?"

"Yes."

"Tell me how you'd get to it."

"From where?"

"From the station. Where else?"

He leaned against the wall. Above him a pop star leered

from a poster.

"Why?" I asked him.

"Bloody tell me," he shouted. "And if you make a mistake," he added, almost conversationally, "you won't make another."

The revolver was pushed painfully against my back, its barrel hitting my spine.

"All right," I said. "When you leave the station you pass Busarus..." I described the route, watching his face as I mentioned familiar streets. He lighted a cigarette and looked away from me. I felt foolishly like a lecturer who has forgotten to bring his slides, and this distraction banished fear as other distractions banish desire. "... so then you turn right", I said, "past Mespil Flats and then left into the hotel."

"That proves very little," he said. "You could have visited Dublin." He was picking at a small blob of dried blood on his cheek. "Are you a Catholic?"

The answer could label me more clearly than anything else I might say. I practised my religion as a child might practise the piano, ignoring it at times and then believing that the five-finger exercises of devotion and attempted prayer might lead to some understanding. I would have denied it without any shame if I had known that this would have helped me. Martyrs must experience a greater degree of hope or of despair than I have ever known.

"Yes," I said, slowly, waiting to see the effect. When he did not say anything I knew that they were not Loyalists. I said, "I wish you'd tell me why I'm here," believing in a cowardly way that I had established some credibility.

"Shut up," he said calmly, the cigarette hanging from his mouth, and the man behind me jabbed the revolver against my spine again as if intent to show that he was still present and more effective than he looked.

"There's somebody coming," the boy called up the stairs. "I can hear a car. Do you want me to look?"

"Keep quiet."

The car went past and I could hear the distant voices of the playing children.

"What are you doing here?"

"Nothing in particular," I said.

He moved quickly and punched me twice in the stomach.

As I fell, the man behind hit me on the side of the head with the revolver. I lay on the floor, conscious of pain and the sound of sniggering and of blood trickling down my face. Some instinct of pride made me get to my feet, swaying drunkenly, attempting to balance as they both hit me again. I remember looking at a pair of shoes and fearing being kicked in the face. The corner of my mouth was bleeding and I wanted to scream but could not; it was as if my tongue had swollen and was blocking the back of my throat. When I looked up and saw the revolver and the faces I feared castration more than I feared death. Mutilated bodies had been found sprawled in ditches along little-frequented roads outside the city. I attempted to push myself upwards, balancing on my hands in a lonely position of love but I fell back on to the floor as if desire had been satisfied.

"Nothing," I said, in humiliation. "A visit." When I spoke I swallowed blood from my lips and believed, for some moments, that I was going to be sick. The shoe stayed near to my face. As I stared, it seemed to assume a character of its own, like a pet animal. For some reason that I do not understand I was tempted to reach out and touch it. Then it moved away and I watched the man in the anorak leave the room. He said something to the boy downstairs and I heard the hall door being closed. The revolver was pointed at me. I tried to wipe blood away from my chin. Some splinters from the floorboards were sticking to my hand.

"You watch it now, do you hear me?"

"Yes."

"Do you think that I wouldn't use this thing? Is that what you think?"

He was not a young man and his hand was shaking.

"I only want to sit up."

"You'd never walk again if I used this, right?"

"Right," I said with some unrealistic hope that I would be able to overpower him. "I just want to sit up." I knelt with some difficulty and became aware of a sharp pain in my side. He moved back, as if I had threatened him. "I'll bloody use it," he said, and the panic on his face was more frightening than anything else had been.

"I haven't got a gun," I said. "You searched me. I just want to sit against that wall." He stared at me intently as if attempting to identify somebody in the dark. "Is that all right?" I asked him. I could see the panic fading from his face and being replaced by a kind of jocular aggression. "You look bloody stupid," he said, and as he giggled I moved back on my knees to the wall and sat beneath a picture of Cliff Richard. "You look bloody stupid. You thought you were a big shot, right?"

"I'm not what you think," I said.

I remember touching my swollen lip and feeling nothing. It was no longer bleeding but my side ached as if something heavy and jagged were embedded there. "All right," he said. "Now stay where you are." He leaned against the opposite wall and lowered his arm, the revolver pointed towards the floor. "You're a silly bloody man," he said in a tone that was almost affectionate. "I wouldn't like to be in your place." I attempted to work out what I should do if I got the revolver. "Don't bloody move," he said as if he had sensed what I was thinking.

The boy came quietly into the room. I had not heard him on the stairs. He peered around as if surprised to discover that I was still there.

"You should be downstairs," the man said.

"I thought you might need a hand."

"If you're found up here . . ."

"Who'd find me? I'd like to beat that bastard," he said about me as if I could not hear. He went to the window and the man watched him anxiously, holding the revolver tightly in his hand. "They should shoot him," the boy said with detachment. "What did he want around here?" He turned from the window and looked at me. "Do you not hear me talking to you?"

"Were you talking to me?" I said, and the shame of my helplessness was like jealousy. I moved to find a more comfortable position against the wall.

"Are you trying to be funny?" he asked.

"Stop it," the man said. Sweat glistened on his forehead. He rubbed the corner of his eye with a shaking finger. "I've been left in charge here," he said without much conviction. "I'm not having anything going wrong."

"He's trying to escape."

I laughed defensively in the way that one might protect

oneself from the implications of an insult. The man stared at me, bewildered, then pointed the revolver.

"If he tries to I know what to do."

"But he's trying," the boy said. "Look at him. He's got to the top of the stairs. You had to shoot him, hadn't you?" Excitement seemed to age him. He stood there in his shabby clothes like someone who has learned too much about life. "I can tell the same story," he said, moving closer to me. "It's the right thing to do."

"I was left in charge," the man said weakly, and I wanted to shout with bitterness at the prospect of such a farcical death. "Listen," I said, "what's the point . . . ?" The contempt in the boy's eyes removed the few tattered remnants of my courage. I said, "Please listen to me," and heard a car door slam. "Oh Jesus," the boy said. He ran from the room and clattered down the stairs. "He's heading for trouble," the man said, as if we were linked by a bond of understanding. "He was warned before. If 'twas known that he left his post . . ." He shook his head and I heard voices from below. The man in the anorak came into the room. "All right," he said without looking at me. "Stand up. No trouble?" he asked as I got unsteadily to my feet.

"None at all."

"And the kid?"

"He's all right."

"He'd bloody better be." He pulled a scarf from his pocket and tied it round my head. "You'd be wise", he said as he knotted it tightly, "to behave yourself. We're going for a drive."

"Where to?"

"Never mind."

He pushed me, and I moved blindly across the room, knocking against the side of the open door. He took me by the elbow and we went down the stairs.

"Will I come?" I heard the boy asking.

"Go home and shut up."

"But I'd like to be there."

"You heard me. Don't argue. Get home."

We went out to the street. I remember wondering if I should shout and realising just how pointless it would be. That was the moment, I believe, at which I felt most futile and most vicious. If I had got the revolver I would have shot all three of them without the slightest regret.

"Get in."

I was pushed into a car and sat there, ineffectually, like a figure in a waxworks. Someone got in beside me and jabbed the revolver melodramatically against my side. "There'll be no talking." Doors slammed; there was a heavy smell of petrol. I was sitting behind the driver. We drove slowly away.

"I've got a right . . ." I said, hardly knowing how I intended to finish the sentence.

"No talking!"

Did I really think about Anna? I believe that I did, after I had given up trying to remember the number of turns that we had taken. The car was an old one; the engine laboured heavily as we went up a hill and something beneath the floor creaked and knocked urgently.

"Turn left," the man beside me said, "that end of the street is blocked."

I remembered kissing her in my car and for a moment I felt the sharp anticipation of being with her again. I shifted on the seat. The revolver came in against my side like an attacking animal.

"I was only . . ." I said, realising that the lack of conversation was worse than the darkness.

"For the last time. Shut up!"

She was the opposite of that; she was some kind of success amongst the failure, she was the only possible argument against a proof of my ineffectuality. I remember thinking, with self-pity: "If I live I won't let you go"; and repeating this over and over again as if it were a prayer.

The car stopped. The man beside me leaned across and opened the door. He pushed me by the shoulder. I got out and listened for traffic sounds. I could not hear any; death seemed to be moving towards me like a presence in the darkness. I wanted to pull off the scarf but before I had found the courage to do so, I was pushed forward. I felt a railings and then, with enormous relief, a door and I knew that I was not standing waiting for death in some lonely country ditch. Someone whispered. I could hear only some of the words ". . . the curtains. Put on the light." For almost a minute afterwards I seemed to be alone. "Can you manage to take off that scarf?" I did not recognise the voice. "It'll probably pull off," he said as I groped at the knot.

The light in the room stung like salt against my eyes. A man of about my own age was looking curiously at me. "Sit down," he said, pointing to a cheap fireside chair. He sat down opposite to me and offered me a cigarette. "The others are outside in the hall." The tone of his voice was not threatening but I could feel my resentment towards him growing like competitiveness. I took the cigarette and looked around the room at an old-fashioned radio set, drawn curtains, pictures of Wolfe Tone and Robert Emmet on the walls, plastic flowers in a vase and some children's toys pushed away beneath a polished table.

"You've caused us a lot of trouble," he said.

"I was walking along a street . . ."

"Take it easy," he said, smiling patronisingly, like someone who knows that an answer can be found by logical progression. "You shouldn't have been walking there."

"It's a free city."

"Is it?" he said. "That's an odd point of view. You'd find very few who'd agree with you."

"You know what I mean."

"And you know what I mean as well. We're getting very sick of pointless walkers." He looked through the papers that had been taken from my pockets. "I don't know much about Davitt," he said, "but I gather he knew what he was talking about."

"If you gathered that you wouldn't be blowing up civilians."

"Not so fast. Civilian casualties have always been an inevitable side effect of any struggle," he said, as if he were quoting from a military manual.

"But it isn't a side effect", I said, "when you pick on nothing but soft targets." I knew that I was doing little to help myself, but his clinical acceptance of other people's wasted deaths provoked me towards argument. "Your struggle has been almost entirely against civilians."

"In an urban situation," he said, "power is defined by the ability to govern. We can make it impossible for anyone at Stormont to govern . . ."

"Without being able to administer real power. Any group

could do what you're doing."

"But without the support of the people . . ." he said.

"Exactly."

He stared across at me angrily but I no longer felt afraid. They were no more brave than I was. I knew his arguments as well as he knew mine. The only worthwhile exchange would have been an honest discussion on motives and long-term plans.

"You have Wolfe Tone on the wall," I said, "but all that you've managed to do, is widen the gap that already existed between the Catholic and Protestant working people."

"That gap was artificially created and preserved by Britain and the Unionist Party." He threw the stub of his cigarette into the empty grate. "And that was the only way that they could occupy this territory."

"That's largely true," I said. "But the IRA and any Loyalist para-military group can only exist as long as that gap does, so it's in all your interests to preserve it."

"Theory," he said with contempt and I noticed, for the first time, a thin white scar that followed the line of his jaw. "I've heard all that theory a thousand times before and it hasn't even started to impress me. If you had to live out your life in a city like this you'd find soon enough that your theory doesn't go very far. If soldiers could come into your house and wreck it on a phoney search in the middle of the night, your theory wouldn't be much use to you. Or if they beat up your wife. Or sent you to a kip like Long Kesh. Or if a Loyalist crowd could burn you out and make sure that you couldn't get a job. And remember that the Loyalists were doing that before we were active again. Would you sit there taking it?" His raised voice resounded amongst the cheap furniture, the plastic flowers. "And you know about the UVF. And you've seen the UDA haven't you? Do you think a Catholic could live in a city like this with a gang like that if they hadn't got us to protect them?"

"That's my point," I said. "You need each other as the only possible justification . . ."

"But the whole establishment will give them support and pretend, at the same time, that democracy can work." He laughed unexpectedly, then leaned forward and said, "Now what about you? Who knows you?"

"I don't know what you mean."

"Who can prove that you aren't working for someone?"

"Can that be proved?"

"It better," he said, "or it's going to be very awkward. You must admit that I've shown a lot of patience."

I looked across his shoulder at the blue and white curtains, the picture of Robert Emmet, the trace of a child's fingers on the wall. He lighted a cigarette and smiled, leaning back on the chair, but there was something about his manner that failed to convince. He reminded me of the false relaxation of someone who is tranquillised.

"Who do you know in Belfast?"

"No one."

"Then what the hell are you doing here?"

"Curiosity," I said, too glibly.

"It's not a fucking peep show!"

"Wait a minute," I said with a return of fear, "I do know someone. He's a journalist called Peter Lawlor."

"Lawlor. How well do you know him?"

"Very well," I lied, and we sat there silently for some moments. I could hear someone whispering in the hall and the insect-like drone of a distant motorbike.

"Peter Lawlor," he said. "All right. If you've been wasting my time your curiosity will cost you more than you bargained for." He left the room, closing the door behind him. I went across to the window and pulled back a section of the curtain, prepared to see anything except the small, neat suburban garden and the playing child. She looked up from the kitten on the lawn and stared towards me with intense preoccupation. I felt strangely guilty, as if I had invaded her privacy. She picked up the kitten and, holding it in her arms, walked towards the window. I let the curtain fall back into place. Someone was talking in the hall. The man in the brown anorak opened the door and said, "All right. Out here."

There were coats thrown across the bottom of the banisters and a reproduction of a galleon in full sail hanging on one of the walls.

"Have a chat," the man said, handing me a telephone receiver.

"Who's on the line?"

"Have a chat."

"Hello!"

"Is that you, Waldron? What in the name of Christ are you doing here?" Lawlor's voice came thin and agitated along the line.

"I wish someone would tell me."

"That *is* Waldron?"

I could not understand his suspicion.

"Of course it is," I said irritably. "What's going on?"

"Where did we meet last?"

"The Europa. You told me about your wife's paintings," I added unnecessarily, as if with a desire to hurt.

"All right. Put me on to whoever's with you. You must be out of your bloody mind."

"He wants to talk to you," I said to the man in the anorak. He took the phone suspiciously.

"Yes," he said. "What? Yes. I'll tell him."

He put the receiver back. "You're a lucky bloody man," he said. "Luckier than you deserve. All right!" he shouted and the older man came from what must have been the kitchen.

"We're going back. Get the mask."

"Do I have to wear it?"

"Is it not fashionable enough for you?" he asked with unexpected humour. He smiled, showing black and broken teeth. I could hear the older man giggling in the living-room, and a child began to cry.

"He doesn't have to see . . ." the older man said when he came out with the scarf.

"No."

"He told you that?"

"He doesn't want to see him again. Put that on him." The scarf was tied round my head and tightly knotted.

"All right. The same regulations. There'll be no chat. Or anything else."

They guided me back to the car.

"Where are you bringing me now?"

"You heard what I said."

To pass the time on the drive I calculated how long it lasted, measuring each second by thinking "one hundred and one, one hundred and two" and keeping a record of minutes with my fingers. I had counted to eleven minutes and thirty-four seconds when the car stopped abruptly.

"All right. Just wait until that woman has gone."

I heard footsteps coming towards the car and wondered what they would do if she saw me and made some comment. The footsteps went past.

"All right."

"Get out," the older man said. I started to untie the scarf. "Get out first and forget you ever met us." I heard the door being opened and I stepped out blindly. The door closed and the car drove quickly away. I pulled off the scarf and saw a brown Renault with tinted windows turn a corner. I had not time to read its registration plate.

I went to the corner and saw that I was near to the station. I wanted a drink and decided to go to the Europa. Then I looked at my watch; the train to Dublin would be leaving in less than five minutes.

Lawlor was waiting at the entrance to the station.

"You must be out of your bloody mind," he said, as if he were still speaking on the telephone.

"Where was I?"

"How would I know?"

"Who were you talking to on the phone?"

"Now listen to me," he said. "If you take my advice you'll shut up. You're a fool to be blundering round here. If they hadn't got through to me, God knows what they'd have decided to do." His agitation seemed a little exaggerated. "It just so happens", he said, more calmly, "that I have some good contacts and they trust me. So I was able to identify you and say that you were harmless."

"Well, thank you very much," I said, and he stared at me uncertainly. I felt no gratitude or warmth. He reminded me too vividly of Anna. It was as if he had stolen something that was mine.

"I'm glad that I was able to help."

"So am I."

He came with me towards the barrier.

"Don't worry about it. They're suspicious of everyone," he said. "But they have some reason to be. You have blood on your face."

"I saw your wife's exhibition."

"Did you?"

"As a matter of fact, I bought a picture."

"Well that's very nice," he said slowly, as if unsure of his own reaction. "I couldn't get away. It was very disappointing to miss it."

"Yes, she told me."

"You've been talking to her?"

"Briefly."

"She didn't mention it. She was on the phone this morning. I'll be down soon," he said. "We must get together then and have a drink."

"I'd like that."

I knew, as I washed the blood from my face in the train, that I was not willing to wait for another day to pass before seeing her. I remembered her crying in my car, and this memory was made vivid by something that was strangely like love. I could even imagine being faithful to her. When I had cleaned my face and my side no longer ached, I went to the bar, filled with unreasonable happiness.

Chapter Seven

She did not answer when I telephoned. I stood there, unhappily, listening to the sound that has often seemed to me to be one of the most emphatic reminders of our isolation. We wait for a voice to come thinly on the line, like someone looking for a miracle, and the ringing tone goes on to wreck our hope. Outside the public telephone box, a small man wearing a ragged coat stared sullenly in at me through the broken glass. I dialled again without any hope, then hung up and held the door open for him.

"This is the fourth one I've tried," he said accusingly. "All the others were broken." He was a little like a porcelain figure from a series of London street criers. "It's a scandal," he said. "I might have to ring for an ambulance." A shrill note of fanaticism was breaking into his voice.

I drove to Pembroke Street and went through the ritual of ringing the bell of her flat. I knew that she was not there. I resented her absence much more bitterly than I resented the scarcely credible events of the day. I wanted her sympathy even more than I wanted her body. It occurred to me, with self-pity, that there was nobody else to listen. An aging prostitute with a sad, over-painted face and broken shoes came round one corner of the square and stood by the steps of an office, clutching her handbag. When she saw me staring at her, she attempted a jaunty smile that became a grimace. I got into my car and drove away, swerving on Leeson Street Bridge to avoid a small girl riding a bicycle.

There were two letters in the hallway. One was unstamped. I hurried upstairs and opened it.

Dear Michael,

I must confess that, in retrospect, I am rather startled by the way that our meeting turned out. I am not usually an impulsive person and I can only wonder why I behaved as I did. I know that you won't be offended if I say that I assume that you have already forgotten that we were supposed to meet again. I am not implying any dishonesty on your part but only being realistic. When you thought about it afterwards – if you thought about it afterwards – you must have realised that there were easier relationships for you. I wish that things were simple and straightforward (as, sometimes at least, they seem to be for other people), but they are not. I must attempt to find a solution by myself, at first, before looking to anyone else to find some sort of happiness. I know that this cannot be clear to you but this is only because there is a factor that I cannot explain. Anyway, I know that it is better not to see you – in case, by any chance, you still thought that we should meet.

When you read this, I will be in Amsterdam where I am going, sooner than planned. I have your book for you safe and will post it to you. I was touched that you still like the picture and hope that you do not hate it now.

                        Sincerely,
                        Anna Lawlor

I read it again, puzzled by its strange defensiveness, and then with a growing predatory pleasure at the involvement that it suggested. I had seen and read indifference too often to be mistaken. Is there a point at which one can say: it was there, it was then that I fell in love? I have never been able to understand love except as a compound of necessities. This is, I know, the thought that a whore might use to justify her function, yet I cannot believe that there is anything corrupt in a fear of loneliness. In that act of mutual failure where love is parodied by strangers one can see real innocence and, as a result, real belief. One goes on hoping that something will change, refusing to recognise that all experiences are as limited as one's own. So if I say that I loved her when I read that letter, I suppose that I am pointing not to her but to an abstraction of my own needs. I remember sitting in the living-room. I could hear news headlines from someone's radio. "In a statement today, the Secretary of State for Northern Ireland . . ." I turned on the television and listened to another expression of tired and pious hopes.

The second letter was from Burgess inviting me to dinner on the following day. "This should be a good opportunity to thrash out some difficulties," he wrote. "I have not been to Dublin before and wish that my stay could be for longer." The book seemed totally unreal, an embarrassment, like some half-forgotten fantasy. I had no more ideas on Davitt, no confidence in my understanding of his motivation. I knew that in the few finished chapters I had simplified him by taking a single idea and pretending to turn it into a man. "In the manner of the worst prose fiction I will carry a copy of a book from the same series, a life of Tom Paine. This should help both of us to avoid those embarrassing, mistaken confrontations."

I cannot remember wondering if I should go to Amsterdam. The plan was formed without questions. But I can remember my happiness as a restoration of confidence. Figures moved and flickered across the television screen, acting out the pitiful, hollow dramas of another day as I thought of walking with her along by the canals, past the gracious old warehouses. Without speculation, I planned destruction and the hopeless months of guilt.

Burgess was waiting for me in the Horseshoe Bar, a small man with a pink and anxious face. He reminded me of illustrations in some book that I had owned in childhood. The life of Tom Paine was placed on the counter beside a glass of gin and tonic. "Oh splendid," he said when I introduced myself, wiping his forehead with a flowered handkerchief and looking around unhappily as if attempting to identify my bodyguards. "No, I've just arrived," he said, and something like a smile flickered for a moment across his broad, smooth face. "I'm still a victim of my first impressions. Taking it all in, I sometimes feel like Isherwood. Real impressions only develop much, much later, in the dark." He spoke quite quickly, as if he were repeating something that had been written for him. "We can put this away now," he said, picking up the book on Paine with marked distaste and putting it into a very new briefcase. "It really wasn't a very happy choice." He looked at his watch, then at me, expectantly, waiting for the next remark.

"It's your first time in Dublin?"

"Yes it is. Isn't that peculiar? I've been meaning to come for years but somehow or other there was always something to prevent it. May I offer you a drink?" he asked and we sat there in silence as he paid for a gin and tonic.

"It's a lovely city," he said, "but what on earth are you doing with your Georgian buildings?"

"Our bureaucrats see it as progress to pull them down."

"They're the same the world over. No feeling for history."

He wiped his forehead again, then tilted the glass in his hand so that the ice chimed against the sides.

"I would have thought that you'd learn from our mistakes," he said. "Poor old London's very sad. The skyline from my office window would make you physically ill. Is that someone you know? She's staring rather hard at us."

I looked across and saw Barbara at a table in the corner. She smiled, then turned to the man who was sitting beside her.

"Yes, vaguely," I said to Burgess. "I can't remember where I met her."

This small deception helped to hide a moment's discomfiture. It was as if I had seen myself, sitting with her, waiting for the time to pass so that we could go to bed. I felt no jealousy, yet her being there had some kind of effect for an aggression, unobtrusive at first, slipped into my conversation.

When we went to the dining-room, Burgess was confessing his political opinions. I use the verb deliberately, for he wiped his forehead and looked around as if he were afraid of being overheard. One might have thought that, like his name-sake, he was planning to defect.

"I'm not doctrinaire," he said. "I don't believe in scientific shifts and that kind of thing. But I'm certainly a socialist in the sense . . ." He paused, as if he had forgotten how his views were formed, his soupspoon held a few inches from his chin. ". . . in the sense that I support freedom and fair play. I don't believe in privileged minorities, do you? Equality of opportunity seems fundamental to me. In the centre of the Labour Party with fellows like Healey and Jenkins you find a balance." He swallowed some soup and frowned. "To tell you the truth," he said, "I'm not at all happy with the kind of books we're publishing in this series. There's one on Guevara that has no balance at all, but the board were convinced that it would sell. And so it has. I think", he said later, "that by and large the Tories are handling the Irish thing rather well. I don't believe that we'd have done substantially better. Degrees of emphasis," he added when he saw that I had not agreed.

"For someone who believes in freedom", I said, "that's a rather eccentric point of view. Britain has made just about every mistake that could have been made. Both parties."

"You're not an IRA supporter?"

"I'm certainly not. Nor does one have to be to see how it's been bungled. But anyone in the IRA would thank you for all you've done to give them support."

I spoke with a nervous vehemence. Barbara had come into the room and was dining with a politician whose ambivalence towards violence was widely known. I could see him in profile, leaning across the table towards her with the easy smile of someone who is almost bored with confidence in their own charm. He put his hand on hers and I heard the familiar laugh.

"Now look here," Burgess said. "I'm perfectly willing to debate with you point by point. But sweeping generalisations belong to Hyde Park. So unless you don't want answers, I'd like to hear how you substantiate . . ."

"All right. Just a few small points. Until 1969, Britain

allowed a deeply sectarian regime to thrive in Northern Ireland. They turned a blind eye to blatant discrimination in jobs and houses. And to gerrymandered constituencies. And to a Special Powers Act that any dictator might have taken as a blueprint."

"There's an element of truth in that," Burgess said with a conscientious fairness that almost made me like him. "But that's the historical background, not the immediate problem. Deeds of omission. You seemed to infer that there had been more recent mistakes. This is excellent roast beef."

"It meant that disloyalty to the state and the freedom that you tell me you cherish were one and the same thing. Anyway," I said, "after the Civil Rights Movement when the old order was falling down and the British Government were finally forced to move, instead of proroguing Stormont, they identified the army and everything they were trying to do with the Unionist Party. Nothing could have been better calculated to create bitterness."

"They *were* the elected government."

"They weren't able to govern. Whatever justification there was for direct rule last March would have been just as applicable earlier."

"Not to Unionist supporters."

"True. But that delay turned the army into the enemy. And when internment was introduced, it was used only against Catholics. That was the final drawing of the line. Is it any wonder that people in the ghettos supported the IRA who pretended that they were there to protect them?"

"That's persuasive simplification," Burgess said. "You seem to think that the suspension of Parliaments and the introduction of laws are matters of expediency."

"Ultimately, they very often are."

"Sometimes, perhaps, but that's not the point. First you've got to make every attempt to establish a fair balance. When there are conflicting or even irreconcilable definitions of what is fair you've got to be pragmatic. A degree of mutual compromise." He drank some wine and said, "Be reasonable. After all, it is a particularly difficult situation. You're speaking with the advantage of hindsight."

"And then there's torture," I said.

"Oh come now!"

"You know a better word?"

"Interrogation?"

"Do you remember Henri Alleg's book?"

"Vaguely."

"Strapped to his vomit-covered board in Algeria? That was interrogation. If you don't condemn all those hoods and those methods of disorientation as they were condemned in France, then I don't see how you can condemn them in Greece or Russia or anywhere else."

I could hear Barbara laughing. The politician had ordered a bottle of champagne and they were drinking a toast. Watching them, I felt a little ashamed of my attack on Burgess. He was smiling good-naturedly.

"The evidence", he said, "is not very strong. If there were conclusive evidence, that would be a different thing. But I don't have to tell you that, even from a distance, it's obvious that a very formidable propaganda war is being fought. On both sides, of course. That tends to blur moral issues."

"Moral issues are usually blurred by expediency."

"Not as I understand politics," he said. "The record of the Labour Government when they were in power . . ."

I watched them with growing indifference. She was wearing her hair in a different way and seemed to be happy. She moved her hand in a gesture that I had forgotten but the memory aroused was blurred. I could remember only my desire for revenge and my jealousy. The politician poured out more champagne and I felt ashamed again. He personified all the ambivalence, all the lack of certitude that made my discussion with Burgess seem hypocritical.

". . . Private Members' Bills on censorship and abortion," Burgess said earnestly. "One can't ignore the evidence of successful democratic agitation."

I offered him a cigarette and our desultory conversation went on. As I thought of Amsterdam it seemed less important to me that people had died on the streets and that a hollow truce was being used to build up support for violence or that Loyalist paramilitary groups were growing up without hindrance, basing their strength on the same old vicious pattern of extortion and murder. Love can make one monstrously selfish. I said, "About the book . . ."

"Oh, yes, of course," he said. He opened his briefcase and handed me the typescript. "I've had it edited," he said. "The comments are in the margin. I believe you'll find them helpful. It's essentially a question of clarity. You can't presume any prior knowledge on the part of the reader. One must" — he folded his plump fingers together — "lock in each fact. This is not an academic work."

"They seem fairly basic," I said.

"Yes, they are. We'll want more on the Fenians. More background. You must use that splendid gift for simplification you've demonstrated this evening." He smiled cheerily across at me like the bearer of good news. "Without falsification, of course. If there's any tension between those two requirements, opt for truth. There's a good chance of paperback sales." He took some photographs from his briefcase. "We're working on the illustrations. I got these newspaper facsimiles from your National Library. This Irishtown meeting," he said, "that seems a key-point. Don't forget to bring that out."

"I'm beginning to doubt that I can write the kind of book you seem to want."

"But of course you can. You almost have in these chapters. You mustn't be offended. If you knew of the editing jobs I've had on some of the series. Bare literacy." He drank some brandy. "You mustn't be at all discouraged."

"All right," I said with something like resignation.

"But you must get a move on. We should have the finished typescript by now."

They left before us. As she walked to the door, she glanced across at me and smiled.

"Nice looking girl."

"English," I said.

"Really?"

He looked after her with a wistful interest, twisting a large, gold signet ring on his little finger. I watched a waiter bow to them with exaggerated deference. The politician had become a most unlikely folk-hero.

"So that's everything," Burgess said. "I think another brandy . . ."

We talked without aggression, drinking more than we should have done as we searched for subjects on which we could agree. Later, I left him, a little unsteady, in the foyer, wiping his forehead and laughing at nothing in particular.

"If others could get round a table," he said, "what a difference it would make."

He was a man who preserved a simple faith in rational solutions.

Chapter Eight

I found a hotel not far from the Rijksmuseum. I had stayed there once before and the proprietor pretended to remember. "Yes, yes, of course," he said, pulling on an old black jacket and giving me a card to sign. "Was it two years ago?" His fingers stirred uneasily across a small pile of tourist street maps. "I just got a cancellation. A nice room. Will you stay long?"

"For a few days at least. Could I book until Thursday?"

"Yes. The weather", he said, "has not been so good but now it is better. A little rain. Would you like a map?"

He showed me to a room with a window looking down on Roemer Visscherstraat. Two girls wearing jeans and check shirts went past to the hostel near the corner.

"All right?"

"Very nice."

"The second key is for the hall door," he said. "I hope you have a very nice stay in Amsterdam."

"I'm sure that I will."

I unpacked quickly as if rushing to keep an appointment. The sun was beginning to appear between the clouds as I went out to the street and walked past the other hotels. I was fully convinced that I could find her in the Rijksmuseum. I hurried along Stadhouderskade quite unaware of anything irrational in the quest. It was half-past three; I knew that the gallery shut at five.

I went up to the second floor and through the series of rooms where guides were leading groups of people from picture to picture. ". . . Philip Korinck's *View with Huts on a Road*. He died in 1688. Can't you see the influence? As with Govert Flinck." For some inexplicable reason that snatch of commentary, spoken in a wavering English voice, remains in my mind. A party of diminutive Japanese wandered unhappily behind a guide, their faces betraying an almost comic sense of incomprehension. I went into the large room where Rembrandt's *Night Watch* is displayed, then up the short staircase to the Vermeers. I thought that I had found her. A girl was standing there, looking at *The Loveletter*. Her back was turned to me but I seemed to recognise the colour of her hair, the line of her shoulder. I watched for a moment, then went across to her, wondering what to say. She turned and walked past me. The unfamiliar face was set in petulant boredom.

I stared at the painting; the austere, translucent colours and the peace. I remember being unable to accept that she was not there. I went into other rooms and disappointment came like a feeling of failure. The guides' voices went on and on as if they were part of a disorientation technique, and the sound of footsteps echoed around the rooms. It occurred to me, for the first time, that we might not even meet. I bumped into a man who was adjusting the focus on his camera; before I could apologise he said, "Bloody clumsy!" then muttered something to a large, perplexed-looking woman who was standing beside him, as I walked away.

I went down the main staircase and waited outside the east entrance. It was twenty to five. I watched each person coming down the steps. A clock chimed the three-quarters and tourist coaches began to pull away. Once or twice I was deceived for a moment as some girl came through the doorway. It was raining lightly and horns were being blown impatiently on Stadhouderskade.

I waited until twenty past five, then walked back to the hotel and had a whiskey in the bar. An elderly Dutchman drank a genever in one corner, stroking his unevenly clipped moustache and staring at the ceiling. I went to my room and attempted to read a magazine, but nothing in it was of interest. I wished that I had brought Anna's letter. Although I could remember the words, I wanted to see them again, in search of a new meaning. There was self-pity in my disappointment and some anger at myself for having assumed that she would be there. The foolishness of the journey was becoming more evident with each cigarette that I smoked.

I have always liked hotel rooms. It is a relief to escape from the things that one uses and collects. I almost relaxed for a while as a pipe gurgled and sighed behind the wall and somebody came down the stairs; footsteps without association. I have never felt lonely in such anonymous surroundings. Loneliness comes with some small aberration from the familiar, not from complete change. The cheap reproduction Paul Gabriel windmill above my bed was as pleasing as any picture that I had ever coveted or bought.

I smoked the last cigarette in the packet and the feeling of relaxation went away. I wanted to see her so much that I almost shouted from the window in adolescent rage. It was as if she had been taken away from me. I wondered, with a new kind of desperation, if she were with another man. This seemed so obvious that I could hardly believe that it had not occurred to me before. There is a factor that I cannot explain. That line from her letter should have warned me.

I went out and walked to a café off Leidseplein. A small band was playing in the square and most of the tables were taken by people who drank glasses of lager as the trams went past. I ordered a meal and attempted to make conversation with a tall, glum German girl. The rucksack she had left beside her chair was covered with national badges. She watched me with dull suspicion, biting into a sandwich and drinking orange juice through a straw.

I loved the city. I suppose it was only then that I began to be aware of it again. I wanted to walk through all the familiar streets, cross the bridges, see the lights in the water. The band played an air that I had heard somewhere before and from a distance the sound of a barrel-organ came like nostalgia.

I finished my meal but continued to sit at the table, drinking lager. My hope of meeting her had been replaced by an equally irrational fear. I thought that if I went to some part of the city that I particularly liked, I would see her there with the other man. I may have been a little drunk. I certainly felt confused. The affair with Barbara had cultivated new depths of suspicion.

"Must you go?" I said to the German girl, who frowned and picked up her rucksack, holding it against her breasts like a baby. She walked away and the bandsmen began to pack their instruments into cases. It was getting dark; coloured bulbs hanging between the trees had been switched on. I asked for another lager and drank it reluctantly. I could see nobody else sitting alone. At the next table, a couple were kissing. Her small, innocent face was covered with surprise when she moved away from him, then she laughed happily and leaned across to kiss him again.

I left the table, intending to return to the hotel. Instead, I walked along Leidseplein, pausing on the bridge across the Keizersgracht to watch a boat come nosing through the water. I did not know what to do.

I went on as far as Kalverstraat, avoiding looking down the Singel towards the Spui and a café in which I had been happy. I thought, sentimentally: If she were with me now it would be so different, aware that nobody else in crowded Kalverstraat seemed to be alone. I went into the American bookstore and looked, without much interest, at the shelves of paperbacks. Upstairs I read some poems by Dunbar . . . although I was slightly drunk I remember the details of this evening more clearly than those of the evenings and nights that were to follow. Perhaps failure sharpens consciousness. I was not lonely but I certainly felt a failure and a little ridiculous as I walked past the big Rokin stores on my way to Dam Square.

The palace was floodlighted. On the steps of the National Monument, a group were singing a peace song and hundreds of boys and girls in shirts and worn jeans were sitting around them listening. I envied something about their self-centredness, their independent confidence and the casual way that reefers were passed from hand to hand. One boy near me reached to the girl who was lying beside him on the steps. She continued to hum the songs as he felt her breasts with clinical interest, like a housewife testing apples in a supermarket. Her jeans were stretched tightly around her thighs; desire came welling through my self-pity as if it were a new sense of purpose.

I went down Warmoesstraat. The spire of the Oude Kerk was gaunt against the sky and I could hear the sounds of trains leaving from the Grand Central Station. As I went along Zeedijk the prostitutes were standing in the doorways of bars. Music blared frenetically from juke-boxes. Two sailors fought ineffectually, swinging wildly at each other until one lost his balance and fell against a wall and then, with a grunt of surprise, to the street. The other went staggering through a red-lighted hall door. A woman stopped beside me.

"Can I show you something?"

"Not now."

"You would like it."

"I'm sure."

She put her hand on her hip like a musical-comedy whore and looked at me enquiringly.

"Something different?"

I did not want her, but on the Oudezijds Voorburgwal I met a girl with a beautiful, dark Indonesian face. If I had taken enough money out with me I would have bought twenty minutes' pretence. I left her regretfully and thought bitterly of Anna as I went towards Damrak to get a tram. A wind came sharply in from the sea and I pictured her with somebody else, relaxed and enjoying herself. "There is a factor that I cannot explain." For some reason, I remembered Lawlor's indignation when we had last met in Belfast. I was not the only one to be betrayed but as I stood on the swaying tram beside a very stout man who was attempting to read an evening paper, this thought brought no comfort.

On the following day I attempted to act as if it were a normal holiday. I walked in Vondel Park, where many of the people who had gathered in Dam Square were still asleep on the grass. It was a bright morning and I felt very little rancour. I was almost happy. I knew that it would not last, but while it did I was anxious to find some perspective that would help when my mood changed. I sat, for a while, near to an ugly statue, then explored some streets around Rembrandtpark, a part of the city that I had not known before. Later, I went back to Kalverstraat and bought some paperback books in the English section of de Slegte's bookshop. I went to a café and glanced through one of them — *A Sentimental Journey* — while having a lager. Should I look for her again? I could not make up my mind and so sat there with the vestige of happiness filtering away.

In the afternoon, I went to the Stedelijk Museum. The new

Van Gogh gallery was almost completed nearby. I looked at the Cézannes but my enjoyment of paintings was blunted, I derived no pleasure from them. They seemed arbitrary and remote. I remember following two middle-aged ladies around to eavesdrop on a conversation that made no sense to me. I wondered what to do next as if it were a duty.

I went down to the restaurant to have a coffee. When I had collected it, I saw Anna sitting by herself at a table. She was flicking through a catalogue. I stood and watched her. There was only one cup on the table and this gave me courage. I went across to her.

"You?" she said, like an intimacy, and it wasn't for several seconds that she looked surprised.

"But what are you doing here?"

"We had an appointment, remember?"

"But that was in Dublin!" she said, laughing. "You couldn't be serious!"

I sat down.

"I am, completely."

"No, tell me," she said, still laughing nervously, pulling at a bracelet that she wore on her left wrist. "What are you doing here?"

"Are you glad to see me?"

"Yes, of course I am." She paused for a moment, as if she regretted having said this. "But you still haven't told me . . ."

"I wanted to see you."

"You couldn't have come all this way," she said with exasperation, but she was smiling. "How could you have known where I'd be? No, tell me," she said when I laughed. "I hate mysteries."

"I got your letter. I wanted to see you so I came here," I said. "It's as simple as that." I reached out and took her hand; it lay in mine like a gift.

"I just don't believe it," she said. "Nobody just decides like that . . ." She took her hand away and said, "There's nothing wrong is there?"

"Not a thing. It's good to see you."

She laughed, shaking her head. She had small, very even teeth and vulnerable eyes. I could feel all the hope that had receded come flowing back.

"But how did you know where I'd be?" she asked again.

"I hoped you'd be here," I lied. "Yesterday when I arrived I went to the Rijksmuseum. I was convinced that you'd be looking at the Vermeers."

"But I was!" she said, delighted, like a traveller in a remote area who encounters someone from their own home town. "I was there for most of the morning."

"I didn't get there until later. What did you do after that?" I asked, half afraid of hearing her answer.

"I came here. Then I went to a cinema. Were you looking for me?"

"Most of the time."

"Isn't that extaordinary!"

"Are you sure that you're glad to see me?" I said, ashamed of the need that I felt for reassurance.

"Of course I am. It's just that I'm so surprised."

"It doesn't spoil your holiday?"

"How could it?"

"Good. I thought from your letter . . ."

"I'll tell you some other time."

This indication of a future and of complicity was like a declaration of love. I remembered kissing her; reaching across possessively I held her hand and we sat there like teenage lovers as the coffee grew cold in the cups.

"How long are you staying for?" she asked.

"I don't know. You?"

"A few more days anyway. I was lonely last night," she said unexpectedly. "Someone tried to pick me up in the cinema. He was very polite and formal. Still it made me feel very much on my own. It's beautiful here, isn't it?"

"Yes."

"I haven't seen that much really. Some of the galleries."

"I'd like to show you places that I know."

"Would you really?" She looked at our hands as if surprised to see them together. "I was going to write to you when I got home."

"Saying what?"

"I don't know. I hadn't worked it out. I'm not good at letters. Why did you want to see me?"

"Because I like you very much." The inadequate words

embarrassed me. Their ungenerous caution made them sound like a rebuke but she laughed and said, "Are you always so impulsive?"

"Never."

"I still don't believe that the only reason you had for coming here . . ."

"Why not?"

"Well, I'm flattered," she said with a little parody bow. "After the last time I didn't think . . ." She looked sadly at our hands. "Were you very surprised when I cried?"

"Not at all," I said, uncomfortably. "Everyone has moods."

"You sound like a therapist."

"Do I?"

We got more coffee and talked for almost an hour in this same inconsequential way. It was as if we were both reluctant to break the mood of our meeting and decide on what to do next. She was more relaxed than I remembered except for occasional interventions of nervousness, when she would stare across at me as if waiting for the answer to a question that she had not asked. I did not tell her that I had met Lawlor again.

We went out to the gardens and looked at some pieces of sculpture.

"We're going to have to decide," she said, after I had kissed her.

"Decide what?"

"I'm not impulsive," she said. "I think I told you that before. I have to know where I'm going and why I'm going there. I don't want to hang on to something insubstantial. Does that make sense?"

"Completely," I said, "but, just for a while, why not take things as they happen?"

"Do you think that's wise?"

"As wise as anything else. I don't believe I've ever made a plan that worked."

She grimaced and I felt a moment of panic at her need for definitions. Then she said, "You're right. I'm far too afraid of the future. I remember not wanting to grow up when I was a child. I couldn't bear the thought of things changing. And still I've always believed in some place better. Not very different but better. What kind of places will you show me?"

"Tomorrow we'll do the grand tour."

"If I went to the gallery in the morning . . . ?"

"I'd meet you for lunch."

"And we must find our own special place," she said happily. "A place that both of us really like, where we can go to every day."

"There's a café in the Spui," I said. "For some strange reason I like it."

"Then you've got to show it to me."

"Where are you staying?"

"In Hooftstraat," she said. "It's handy. I'm glad that you came," she said later when we were waiting for a tram. Offices were closing and businessmen walked importantly along the pavement as if they were in a procession. "I'm only getting used to the idea now."

"Thank you for being glad."

"Were you sorry when you missed me yesterday?"

"Very."

I almost told her about the kind of evening that I had spent but decided against it. I kissed her, grateful for not being alone any more, remembering the Indonesian girl with only faint regret. In her shirt and old jeans she looked a little like the girl I had coveted in Dam Square and I wanted to touch her breast when the tram came along. We got in and stood close together.

"I've learned the numbers off by heart," she said. "They're very easy to follow. I'm usually lost in any city but Dublin. You haven't been to Belfast since?"

"No."

"It's odd not to read about it every day. I saw a picture of Brian Faulkner in a paper yesterday."

"Let's go to dinner," I said abruptly, hoping to change the subject.

"That's not a bad idea."

If she had thought of Lawlor — and she must have done so — it had made no difference. Her mood did not change. She was, I learned later, a person of disconcerting honesty with almost none of my own inclinations towards self-protection. She told the truth about herself and her feelings except when the details of her marriage were involved. Then she was at least reticent.

We went to the Dorrius Restaurant. "Our place is just a stone's throw away," I said. "I'll show it to you later on so you'll know where to meet me tomorrow."

"Good. It's nice here," she said. "Will they mind my wearing jeans? Isn't it just like a picture of a London club?"

We both enjoyed the meal. Later, when we were drinking coffee, she said, "Look, I have to talk. I just can't go on wondering . . ." She pulled at the bracelet nervously, and refused a cigarette. "You want to sleep with me, don't you?"

"I'd like to very much."

"All right," she said. "I'd like it too. But there's something . . ." She paused, disconcerted. I did not know what to say so I remained silent. "It's private, isn't it?" she said slowly. "I wouldn't ever want Peter to know."

"Yes, of course it is. Why wouldn't it be?"

The waiter came over to the table to pour us more coffee and we sat in a kind of truce, not looking at each other until he had gone.

"Of course it's private," I said. "Who would I want to tell?"

"I didn't mean you'd talk about it. I just wanted to be sure we wouldn't be . . . found out. I've never had an affair," she said. "Not since I was married."

"I think that I love you," I said. The idea of her marriage was like a rival.

"No, please," she said, "let's say 'like' until we're certain. I certainly like you."

"I'm in like with you," I said and she laughed. "It's like that makes the world go around."

I think back on this conversation with real sadness. It was sad, I suppose, even at the time. Hopes built on such tenuous acquaintanceship are far too vulnerable to small accidents; misunderstood words, gestures and expressions misread, even minor changes of mood.

"Where will we go?" she asked.

"My hotel isn't bad . . ."

"No, you come back to mine."

"Tomorrow we can book in somewhere."

"It's a small room," she said. "And the bed isn't very big, but it's nice enough."

The intimacy of our plans were even more exciting than

the thought of imminent lovemaking. Her knee rested against mine; I reached beneath the table and touched her thigh, proprietorially. She blushed, holding her coffee-cup and said, "I'm very shy. I always have been. Is that unusual? I talk a lot when I'm nervous. I wouldn't mind a drink", she said, "before we go. But tomorrow I buy us dinner. After all, some of the money I've got is the money you spent on my painting."

"I like you, Anna."

"Do you?" she said. "I like you."

I ordered brandy.

We sat in silence for a while, watching a man read a copy of *De Telegraaf* at one of the reading tables that made the restaurant seem so much like a club. He took some snuff from a box, spreading it on the back of an old and shaking hand before inhaling it deeply.

"I'd like to paint him," she said. "Look at the way his head comes tumbling off his neck as if it were too heavy!"

He picked up his paper again.

"But I haven't the technique yet," she said.

"Your own self-portrait. Surely the technique in that..."

"No, no," she said. "Not at all. I cheated. I didn't even try to paint what I saw in the mirror. I made it easy."

I knew nothing of the sources of her talent and felt excluded. One begins by loving simple things. The details are filled in later to add to the early feeling or destroy it.

"I can't imagine you cheating," I said.

"There are lots of ways." She drank some brandy. "But at least I'm ashamed when I do it. Some people make a virtue of it, even when there's no necessity. I won't do that."

We left and went to the Spui. "That café there," I said. "When you see it in the daytime... Can that be our special place?"

"It is already. I like it. Why don't we walk?"

"Are you sure?"

"Yes, let's. It's a lovely evening."

A barrel-organ was playing on Leidsestraat, pumping out a loud and jaunty tune. We stopped and joined a small crowd to listen.

"It's like no other sound," she said. She took out some change and gave it to a grey-haired man who was making a collection. He had a monkey on his shoulder. "I never knew they were so big," she said.

The carved, wooden organ was hitched to a van and driven by a motor.

"Yes, big," the man said and the monkey squinted suspiciously at us, rattling his chain as he scratched his mangey chest.

"Still," she said to me, "it's a sad kind of sound somehow, isn't it, even when the music is cheerful?"

"I think so too."

We looked into some shop windows.

"I'm delaying us," she said. "I've only realised it now. It isn't that I don't want to arrive . . ."

"You prefer to travel hopefully?"

"In a way," she said. "I suppose that's probably true. I keep on asking myself what will change and I haven't got an answer. But it's what I want. I won't delay us again," she said smiling, "and I won't go on thinking out loud."

"I like to hear you thinking," I said.

"This time tomorrow."

"What about it?"

"I don't know," she said. "I'm still thinking out loud. I'm going to stop now. That's a promise."

"It's no wonder you're afraid of the future if it's always weighing on your shoulders."

"Do you know what you'll feel?"

"I don't even want to," I said. "I know what I feel now."

"So do I," she said. "And I believe in tomorrow."

Chapter Nine

"Is it all right?" she asked me as if I were there to rent it from her.

"It's very nice."

There was a sketchpad on the single bed and a large red suitcase left open near to the door.

"Are you sure?"

"Yes, certain."

"There's a bolt on the door," she said. I went across and pressed it stiffly into place. She put the sketchpad on a table. I took it and began to flick through its pages; faces, a small girl standing on the deck of a houseboat, cats and windows.

"No, don't," she said, taking it from me. "They're only doodles. I'll show you if I do anything good but until then I don't want you to see . . ." She put it into the wardrobe. "It means so little," she said. "It embarrasses me to have anyone else see it."

The sound of coughing came from the room next door.

"Last night I could hear him snoring."

"Did you knock on the wall?"

"How could I?" she said, laughing. "Anyway it wasn't all that loud. I was lying awake." She closed the suitcase and tidied some cosmetics on the dressing-table.

"He'd better not start again!"

"I hope", she said, "that you don't think it's too squalid here. I haven't looked at it carefully before."

"It's not in the least squalid," I said, looking down to the broad street and the passing cyclists and an old lady who limped slowly along with a dog in her arms.

"Still, I wish it were home," Anna said. "Not an hotel room."

She came to the window. I put my arm around her.

"Do you know what I mean?"

I did but I said, "It doesn't make any difference. We're together. That's all that matters. And anyway I like hotels. And I like you."

"I like you."

We undressed and got into bed. She was trembling; her body was very cold. When I tried to hold her the trembling got worse and she said, "I'm sorry. I'm sorry." I could see the panic in her eyes.

"Don't worry," I said. "If you don't want . . ."

"I do!" she said, almost angrily. "It isn't that, I promise."

We talked for a while, awkwardly. I could feel her tension coming into me like a sense of foreboding. I tried to amuse her and failed. We lay coldly together like old enemies.

"It'll be all right later," I said.

"No, soon," she said, as if she were pleading. "Soon. It'll be all right soon. I know it's silly."

I warmed her hand in mine, feeling the fingers flex and jerk like nerves, and her body remained rigid as tears replaced the panic in her eyes.

"What would help?" I asked as gently as I could, afraid that my desire would be replaced by irritation.

"Please hold me," she said. "You must think me so stupid."

"No I don't," I said. "Whatever it is it's *you*. And I like you, remember?"

She kissed me hesitantly. I held her in my arms and when she no longer trembled, we made love very badly and without pleasure. She gave a small cry of pain as we moved inadequately Afterwards she asked, "Was it all right?"

"Of course it was."

"Are you sure?"

"Certain."

I could not understand her search for reassurance. Her disappointment must have been as intense as mine.

"I'm sorry," she said, "that I was so . . ."

"Don't be sorry," I said, kissing her. "Why should you be? It takes a little time."

I went to the bathroom and threw away the sheath. When I came back to the bed she was smiling. "I didn't think I would," she said. "I'm glad that I did."

"Why did you think that you wouldn't?"

"Doubts. I haven't got very much confidence. When I wrote in the letter that there was a factor . . . that was what I meant. I haven't had much experience," she said abruptly. "You must see that."

"Don't be defensive for no reason," I said. "I like you."

"And don't patronise me."

"Was I patronising you?"

"No," she said. "Of course you weren't. I'm sorry."

We held each other but unease spread like a mood of depression between us.

"I'm sorry," she said. "If you only knew how little I meant what I've said. Or the way that I've said it."

"I know."

"How could you?"

We lay there like people in a half-remembered dream. There seemed to be no logic in the sequence of moods as if other happenings had been forgotten. I found myself waiting for the panic with which so many of my own dreams have ended as I stroked her face and attempted to reassure her.

"Do you mind if we dress?"

"No," I said.

We went out to a café and I bought a bottle of wine. When we were both a little drunk, she said, "I've never slept with him, you see."

"With who?"

A tram went silently past and an American couple sat at a table near to us. They spread bags and parcels across it and the woman shouted, "Waiter!" as if she were shouting "Help!"

"With Peter."

"Why not?" I asked.

"Don't say it like that."

"I'm sorry. I just meant why not."

I reached for her hand but she moved it away impatiently.

"It's a simple question."

"No it's not."

"Then don't bother," I said resentfully, ignoring the implications of what she had said. I ordered more wine and waited for the fight that I was certain we were going to have. When the waiter went away I saw, guiltily, that she was crying.

"I'm sorry, Anna."

She shook her head and turned away from me, like a child convinced that grief is inconsolable. The Americans talked loudly at each other. They might have been having different conversations, each unaware of the other's interjections. The air was becoming cool as the sky darkened.

"I'm sorry, Anna."

"It doesn't matter."

"Please tell me about it."

"What else is there to tell?" she said. "Just that."

"But there must be more than that," I said, spilling some wine that bled across the table towards her. "You can't just leave it at that."

We were both a little drunk, yet I wince when I remember my own insensitivity. She had changed into a dress that made her look older and less attractive. When I recall my words I can hear again a note of impatience even in my apologies. Some wine dripped on to her knee and she wiped it with her fingers.

"I've always valued privacy," she said.

"So have I."

"Not just my own. Other people's as well."

"Do you think that I'm different?"

"How would I know?" she said with what might have been bitterness.

"I like you," I said foolishly.

She grimaced. "Do you?"

I reached across the table to take her hand and wine soaked coldly into my sleeve. Her fingers lay like a plaster-cast in my hand as desire returned, unprompted.

"Very much. Please tell me as much as you want to tell and not a syllable more."

"Well, I've told you really," she said. "We haven't made love. Properly. I don't know why but I don't think that it's my fault."

"You mean that he can't?" I avoided using his name.

"Or won't," she said. "I don't know. We tried a few times and then postponed it. It's very difficult to explain. Then he went to Belfast and somehow or other . . ." She wiped some tears from her face and said, "I used to hope . . ."

"Why did you stay with him?"

"I love him."

"Even though . . ."

"Of course," she said indignantly. "It'll work out."

"Do you believe that?"

"I don't know. A lot of the time I don't even think about it. He was going to go to a psychiatrist," she said, "but I don't think that he did. I've never told anyone. I don't know why I'm telling a stranger now."

This was meant to hurt me and it succeeded. I looked away resentfully at the busy street. An old man with war medals pinned across his coat went by on crutches. He muttered obsessively to himself as he swung along like some ancient mechanical toy.

"I didn't mean strangers that way," Anna said.

"I don't mind. I know what you mean."
"Does it all seem grotesque?"
"No. Sad. It mustbe lonely for you."
"Sometimes."
"If I had known this evening I'd have been more . . . gentle."
I said, "I assumed . . ."
"How could you have known?"

The conciliatory tone embarrassed me and when she reached out her hand I took it with a faint reluctance.

"Perhaps it's my fault," she said.
"You mustn't think that."
"It's a possibility. I can't be certain, you see."

Her hand was trembling. I could scarcely remember the details of her naked body except for the shape of her breasts and the colour of the broad, bruised nipples.

"Let me help," I said meaninglessly, with a sense of impending shame. "Are you sorry that I came?"
"No. Glad."
"Are you sure?"
"Yes. And you?"
"Very glad."
"Really?"

We reassured each other and drank more wine. A light rain was falling. I remembered how desperately I had searched for her and feeling something like gratitude, said, "I was lonely before I found you."

She did not reply. Rain dripped from the awning above our heads to the top of the table.

"It's getting late," she said. "Just for tonight I'd prefer if we didn't . . ."

"That's all right," I said with some relief. "Don't bother trying to explain."

"Are you sure? Just for tonight."

Her own relief spread like happiness across her face. "Am I a coward?" she asked, almost cheerfully. "But tomorrow will be different. I know. It was bound to be difficult. I should have told you before." She finished the wine in her glass and smiled. Her cheeks were flushed. I might have believed that she had a sense of fulfilment if I had not shared in her failure.

"Don't give up on me now," she said as if I had betrayed

the first small signs of retreat.

"Not a chance," I said. I could easily believe that I was in love with her. "So tomorrow's all right?"

"At lunchtime? In our special place?"

"Will you know how to get there?"

"I'll find it."

"Are you sure?" I asked, already beginning to doubt that I would see her again. "On the Spui?"

"I remember."

We walked back to her hotel. The sense of a permanent parting was reinforced by the way that we stood on the pavement in the light, warm rain. I was reluctant to leave her yet could not have managed another ordeal of reassurance.

"All right," she said, "I'll see you tomorrow."

"All right."

We did not even kiss. I am fatalistic enough to have doubted that there was any potential for happiness between us. I remember thinking that love would go sour from tension and suspense. I did not anticipate our happy moments but neither did I suspect the depth of unhappiness that lay ahead. Our past is populated by strangers. I look back with irritation at my own inability to see the future, at a barely recognisable figure who stolidly blunders on like a man under orders to leave the trenches.

"Until tomorrow," she said, with a strangely intimidated air.

"Until tomorrow."

I arrived too early at the Café Hoppe. There was almost an hour to pass before I could expect her. I waited for a tram to go by, then crossed the road to the Athenaeum bookshop. There were new posters in the windows urging support for obscure revolutions. I went inside and looked through back numbers of little magazines, watching the girls who went up and down the stairs with the clumsy yet exotic grace of the young and committed. In their concern for Guinea and Paraguay, they would have found my ideas pathetic; my cautious belief in socialism and the chance of a peaceful solution in Northern Ireland.

When the time had passed I sat at a table outside the café and waited. It was warm and only a few thin clouds were webbed across the sky. The next door bar was busy. Some men came out with sandwiches and stood on the pavement, chewing laconically and staring without much interest at the people who passed. A man with a basket of fish fixed to the handlebars of his bicycle stopped nearby. A woman bought a trout and for a surprising moment I could smell the sea.

When I saw her coming across the street I felt a strong relief as if her presence exonerated me from some responsibility that I had feared. She was wearing a long green dress and she smiled.

"Am I late?"

"Not at all. But still I was afraid that you wouldn't turn up."

"Were you?" she said. "It was never in doubt. I thought a lot last night." The cane chair creaked as she sat down beside me. "About us. I don't see why other circumstances should affect what we feel now. Or what we do. I've always been cheated by worry and consequences. I want to be free to feel something more than a vague sense of guilt that I shouldn't be doing what I'm doing. Does that make sense?"

"Of course," I said doubtfully. Her innocence was like a challenge. We ordered sandwiches and lager and created involvement, step by step, as if we were making some kind of final effort to save a marriage. She offered herself like a pupil and I found myself speaking with an authority that I did not feel.

"I could learn to be a good lover."

"Of course you could," I said.

"If you have patience."

"That's not necessary."

"It is with me."

There was something asexual about the prospect and yet I wanted her; wanted to hear her cry out beneath me in shared pleasure. I touched her hand and she told me about some of the pictures that she had seen and liked.

"That picture you bought," she said later. "I want to buy it back from you. It isn't real. Or if it is it's only the reality of a tear. There's nothing enduring about it."

"Except the emotion that produces a tear," I said. "That can last."

"Self-pity," she said. "I'll paint you something that has nothing to do with feeling rejected in the middle of the night. I'll never be a great artist. I discovered that years ago but I'll try to be more than competent."

"How can you know?"

"I'd be a fool if I didn't," she said. "Where will we stay?"

"A new hotel."

"Yes. Somewhere beside a canal where you've never been before."

We found a room in a small hotel in Bloemgracht. The ceiling sloped towards the window and the bells of a church in the next street whirred and groaned into action every quarter of an hour. There were trees across from our window and then the canal with barges moving slowly like matrons through its grey-green waters.

"This is ours," Anna said as if I had found her a home. I remember being embarrassed at the new definition of our roles. The cases lay on the bed like evidence, the large, old-fashioned key of the room beside them.

"You like it?"

"Very much," she said. "Don't you? Oh, please don't be disappointed!"

"I'm not in the least."

"Good. I'd like to live here," she said. "In a room like this. Do you think it would cost a lot? I could get some kind of job. But that's nonsense," she added as if rebuking a younger self. "I can't, so what's the point of fantasizing? What do you want out of life?"

I was tempted to choose an easy answer but the real enquiry in her tone made me think for some moments. "Not to be entirely anonymous," I said. "An egotistical ambition. To have my privacy and some rights to a small corner of the world. Some men want sons for that reason."

"Don't you?"

"Not particularly."

"I'd like a child," she said, and I saw with irritation that I had blundered back into the reality of her world.

"A reflection of yourself?" I asked her, for there was no point in attempting to change the conversation.

"No. An opposite. Surely the whole fascination would be in seeing someone you might have been but are not. A piece of yourself that's free from all the accidents that made you what you are."

"But trapped in a new series of accidents."

"Or, liberated by them. Like a soul that's saved. Did you ever wonder", she asked me much later as we ate our dinner in a students' café, "what it would have been like to have had one different parent? Just one?"

"Which one would you change?"

"I don't know."

She sat across from me, her chin supported on her hand, giving my casual question more consideration than it deserved. "I suppose... my father," she said. "It isn't that I didn't love him, but I suppose I was disappointed that he wasn't different. More important. Even as a child I could never understand why he wasn't more... decisive. He seemed to apologise for what he was and that made him a little unreal. Like some kind of Old Pretender who's been cheated of the crown."

"Is he dead?"

"Yes. He died when I was twelve."

The sound of a juke-box boomed through the café and a couple began to dance between the tables. The guttural words of the song seemed more expressive of hate than of love but the music suggested sentimentality. I remember hoping that she would not want to dance.

"And your mother?"

"She's alive. She's a very strong person. Not well educated but sure of her own beliefs. I think that watching her gave me any confidence that I have. We own a small farm," she said. "She runs it much more efficiently than my father did. I remember him telling me once that he felt defeated by the predictability of the seasons. But my mother likes to make a success of things. She never liked Peter. The first time that I brought him home to meet her she was almost rude to him. I cried."

She told me about her childhood; a small girl sitting on a wall, staring at her father and inventing brothers and sisters from pieces of rope and paper bags crayoned as faces. One evening she had found her father lying face downwards in a field. She had crept up silently and pounced, laughing and calling, but he had not moved. Her mother, she said, had expressed no regret. At the funeral, when neighbours commiserated with her she had said, "His will be done."

We went back to the hotel. The reflection of lights broke and re-formed on the surface of the dark canal, and seagulls wailed like anguish. A large moth flew blindly around our room, bumping noisily against the walls and flattening its wings on the ceiling. Anna used her sketchbook to push it out of the window.

When we had undressed, she insisted on pointing out her body's minor imperfections, speaking as clinically as if she were using a chart at an anatomy class. When I protested, she said, "I wanted you to know that I know." This seemed so unreal that I started to protest again, but she covered my mouth with her hand.

"No, don't," she said. "You'd have noticed and naturally not have said anything and that would have been the first secret barrier between us."

"But I think you're beautiful," I said through her fingers.

"I'm glad that you do," she said.

The bed creaked lugubriously. The smallest movement was magnified to sound like passion.

"How could one live in sin", she said, "without a creaking bed?"

"Comfortably."

"I think that I'd have felt cheated without it."

"I like you."

We made love more skilfully than before. Her eyes lost some anxiety as we moved to the ludicrous creaking, and afterwards we spoke undefensively about how it could have been better. I remember holding her in my arms as the clock chimed three times. She was almost asleep. We lay together in an attitude of trust. "I knew", she said, "that today would be different. Didn't I tell you? I knew it would be different."

Chapter Ten

I endangered the morning with a casual and over-confident remark.

"When I met Peter in Belfast," I said, "he told me that you were very much in love."

She turned away from me. We had made love and were lying on the crumpled cover of the bed. Her defenceless back and the soft curve of her buttocks aroused my desire again but I saw that she was crying.

"Anna."

"Please don't touch me."

"I'm sorry."

"Why did he say that?"

"I don't know. I suppose that he meant it."

"But what was the context?" she asked. "He wouldn't say anything like that just out of the blue." She brushed at the trail of tears with her fingers. "What business had you talking about it at all?"

"I must have seemed puzzled that he was in Belfast and you were in Dublin. What a stupid thing for me to have told you!"

"It was nice of him to say it," she said.

"Nice of him?" A sense of rivalry came like a sudden fear and it was cowardice more than caution that prevented me from attacking him bitterly.

"Yes, nice of him," she said. "I'd have told you the same thing. Anyway, it was true once."

"Is it true now?"

"Only partially," she said.

"I could bite my tongue out."

"Don't," she said. "I enjoy it very much."

We laughed, but an undercurrent of unease remained. A tram-bell rang in the distance.

"Don't let it spoil . . ."

"How could it spoil anything?" she said quickly.

"I've got a habit of jeopardising what I've got," I said. "Spoiling it in case it's taken from me."

"I hadn't noticed."

She went to the gallery. When I met her at lunchtime I knew that the danger had passed. After lunch we visited the Anne Frank house. I saw tears in her eyes when she looked at the faded pictures of Hollywood stars cut from magazines and pasted on the walls of the room that the girl had shared with Dussel.

"Her little fantasies," she said, "when she was witnessing the putting into practice of the biggest fantasy of all."

"You've read the diary?"

"Several times."

An elderly man said, "Discrimination is only starting in our time. If anyone thinks we learn anything from the past they better get their head examined."

His old, black face was crumpled and brittle and his bloodshot eyes stared sightlessly ahead. The woman with him looked embarrassed.

"If any of my people had been taught to write, what kind of diaries would they have left? Do you think that the whole black world . . . ?"

"That's the object of our Foundation," somebody said. "Wherever there's hatred or discrimination . . ."

"Let's go," Anna said. "There's something frightening about this house."

"Don't tell me about Foundations. What use are Foundations to a girl of six who's been raped?"

"If we fight against prejudice first . . ."

"I'm not talking about prejudice! That's an abstraction. I'm talking about what's real."

"Could you ever hate anyone?" she asked me when we were outside the house. Light seemed to be trapped on top of the tower of the Westerkerk; it glistened like a jewel.

"I suppose that I could."

"But you never have?"

"Hate is too strong a word."

"What would somebody have to do?"

"See through me," I said, and although I was joking I realised that it might be partially true. "Or take you away from me. Have you ever hated?"

"I don't think so. I imagine it's even more difficult than love."

"And possibly more rewarding. Its continuation doesn't demand reciprocity."

"You don't mean that!"

I remember the expression on her face, the conflict of disapproval and laughter. That was a moment of unusual happiness. We leaned against a railing by the canal and kissed until somebody passing on a bicycle whistled mockingly.

"I love you," I said.

"I love you."

"I want you."

"Me?" she said, assuming the open, innocent pleasure of a child.

In my memory of the next three days we move in slow-motion. I see her on a bridge, looking down at a seagull in the water. She is stepping on to a barge where a flowerseller hands her a rose. We are dancing in the 44 Club and the clasp of her necklace breaks. Small red and white beads go bouncing slowly through moving feet. Her laughter expresses astonishment. I see her coming out of Rembrandt's house not certain of why she feels disappointed and walking between the stalls in dull, grey Waterlooplein, humanising the junk by her interest. When she cries, the tears seem impossibly small and her pleasure is almost soundless. The picture from *The Irish Times* reminds me of her face.

"We have to go soon," she said.

We had taken a canal boat and were out in the harbour where huge, clumsy ships were dry-docked and being repaired.

"I suppose so."

"Do you mind going home?"

"I haven't got much to go home to."

"The thought of it frightens me," she said.

"You're not to be frightened."

The boat swayed erratically as it met a new onslaught of waves.

"Why should you be frightened?"

"I just am."

"Of Peter?"

"No, of myself, I suppose. It's bound to be different."

"Not between us."

"But it must be," she said. "This isn't the reality of life for either of us. You know that. So please don't pretend..."

"Why shouldn't it be our reality?"

"It's one part of our lives," she said. "We'll move on to others."

"Would you leave him?"

She hesitated, and I found that I was not certain of the

answer that I wanted to hear.

"I don't suppose that I would."

"You could easily get a separation. It hasn't been a marriage."

"Yes it has. In other ways," she said. "There are other ways."

"But you love me?"

"Yes. That doesn't mean that I'm going to change everyone's life," she said, and I found that beneath my jealousy of Lawlor there were some stirrings of relief. I did not know if I wanted to marry her. I could more easily imagine the satisfactions of a long, conventional affair.

"I'm not going to let you go," I said. "We've too much to share together. Happiness is scarce."

"It's the furtiveness I'd find most difficult, in a place like Dublin," she said. "All one's energies could be involved in avoiding living out the truth."

"As yours have been. Negatively."

"It's not difficult to pretend that you're happy. People assume it. They take it for granted unless you look battered or become known as some kind of addict. They don't care. But the thought of secret appointments and being afraid to answer the door . . . I think that would spoil everything. It would be corrupt."

"Except that it needn't be as furtive as that. He's in Belfast."

"He has friends in Dublin."

"Even if he did find out," I said, "he could hardly blame you. Does he expect you to opt for sublimation for the rest of your life?"

"I don't want him to know," she said with unusual finality. The boat was turning in from the harbour and the lights of the city were spread softly ahead. We passed a Japanese freighter; sailors standing at a rail, like the chorus in a musical comedy, looked down at us and grinned.

"We can plan it so that it isn't furtive."

"Do you think so?"

"I *know* that we can."

I put my arm around her. She was cold and pressed against me as if seeking refuge from some fear.

"I'd like that," she said. "I was often too lonely. Tell me about the last girl that you loved."

"I didn't love her."

"The last girl you slept with then. What was her name?"
"Barbara."
"Was she good in bed?"
"I can scarcely remember," I said.
"No, tell me. I'd like to know."
"I suppose that she was."
"Were you nice to her?"
"Yes," I lied. "Why do you ask?"
"Just to know something about you. Was she beautiful?"
"No. She doesn't interest me now," I said. "Why would she interest you?"
"I'd be very jealous", she said, "if you slept with someone else while we're . . . doing it."
"So would I."
"If I did? Would you really? The most hurtful thing of all, I suppose, would be if you didn't care. To be minimised would be awful. I suppose it's because I've felt rejected for so long. Although it isn't actually rejection, the effect is the same. I feel ugly and awkward. He's really very kind and generous with everything except his time. I like him very much. I don't want to hurt him."
"He won't know. You overestimate the need for secrecy. Discretion is all that's needed."
"Perhaps you're right."
"I know that I am."
"Then you're right!"
The tall, seventeenth-century houses loomed up on each side of the canal. They seemed one-dimensional in the evening light, like old woodcuts.
"That house we saw," she said. "Anne Frank's. I didn't like it."
"Why not?"
"It was just too pathetic and then that man shouting. It didn't seem right to be there. And I wanted to feel something but all I could feel was a kind of repulsion. It was like eavesdropping."

We postponed making love. The pleasure of anticipation grew more keen as tensions disappeared. We undressed and talked, lying on the bed, drinking sharp, red wine from paper cups. She showed me some pages from her sketchbook. I remember the face of an old man, drawn so lightly in pencil that I felt it would smudge into powder if touched.

"He was sitting in the Rijksmuseum," she said. "I think he was asleep. These are just preliminary things." She flicked over the pages; hands and heads, a boy with a crutch, a girl lying on the grass, her legs spread wide, one hand beneath her head.

"That's just an exercise," she said. "I didn't see her. These are some of the houses and a bridge. That bridge might be a painting. I like the imperfection of the arch."

The sketchpad lay on her stomach. She frowned down at it in an effort of concentration, unaware of my inability to wait any longer.

"I want you."

These inadequate words always seem foolish to me when I hear my own voice speaking them. Like the articulation of so many other emotions, they fail to convey any conflict. Desire is so often a tension between an urge towards tenderness and aggression. There was something about her naked body that made her more vulnerable than any woman whom I had ever known. A certain awkwardness in the way that she moved, a sense of half-suppressed feeling, aroused me more than practised expertise had ever done. I have just remembered that she would always push at my shoulders and stare up into my face before allowing me to enter as if to reassure herself that she was not lying beneath a stranger. At those moments her eyes were expressionless but her fingers were always pressed tightly into my skin and the pain that she unconsciously gave became part of my pleasure. I never told her this. We stay trapped in our worlds, sending signals out into space, aware that the end of our isolation could be perilous. She pushed the sketchpad to the floor and lay as passive and remote as the girl that she had drawn. Her eyes were closed but when I touched her she turned and moved against me and we made love urgently as if it were a last act of defiance.

"Am I as good as Barbara?"

"Much, much better," I said. "I love you."

"I'll learn."

"Think of all the time that we'll have. It will never be furtive."

Chapter Eleven

I was waiting for her in the Spui when I saw a man come out of the Athenaeum bookshop and glance at his watch. At first, I thought that I must be mistaken. A lorry came from Spui Straat, blocking him from sight, but when it had passed he was lighting a cigarette and I could see the sallow face, the long, thin scar along the jaw. The memory of Belfast was vivid; the small suburban living-room with its patriotic pictures and cheap furniture and this man asking questions.

I left a guilder on the table and followed him across a bridge and down Herengracht. There were cars parked along the cobbled street; it would have been simple to duck behind one of them if he had turned. He walked quickly, smoke trailing from the cigarette in his hand. He looked at his watch again. He might have been a businessman, quickening his step to reach some office in time for an appointment. A barge called the *Kenneth Demcy* passed slowly along the canal and a girl on a bicycle came wobbling towards us.

At the intersection of Rhaddastraat he paused because of the busy lunchtime traffic. I stood behind a tree until he had crossed, then followed him, afraid that he would turn to look when a Renault had to brake sharply to avoid me. But he went quickly down Herenstraat and across towards Prinsengracht and the streets that I knew well. I widened the gap between us when I was no longer afraid of losing him so that even if he had turned he would not have seen me.

Although the pursuit had little purpose, I began to enjoy it. It seemed to make some amends for the humiliation of our previous meeting. He threw away the cigarette and walked even more quickly. My enjoyment increased.

Along this section of Prinsengracht, a jumble of houseboats were moored. Some were obvious homes, brightly painted, with potted plants and curtains in the windows. Others were more nondescript; on some of these pornographic shows were held in the evenings and one was a brothel.

The man stopped and a cat went streaking across to the open

door of a house. From the shelter of a tree, I watched as he stepped on to the polished deck of a houseboat. It looked like the home of an elderly, houseproud couple; there was washing on a line and a canvas-backed chair on the deck, a newspaper spread across the seat. He looked around for the first time, then knocked at the door and said something that I could not hear. After a few seconds he knocked again and the door was opened by Lawlor.

They spoke for a few moments, then went into the cabin and the door was closed. I believe that I waited there for ten or twelve minutes or perhaps for even longer. I kept staring at the cabin door as if someone would come bursting through it with a rifle aimed at the tree. The washing swayed slightly in the breeze and some pages of the newspaper stirred, but when nothing else happened I grew bored and walked slowly towards the Spui.

Anna was waiting there. I did not tell her about what I had seen. We were leaving on the following day having changed our tickets so that we could be on the same flight.

"We must do something special tonight," she said.

"Of course. What would you like to do?"

"I'll think," she said, and I found myself looking anxiously at everyone coming towards us. Their anonymous faces appeared to accuse me.

"Is anything wrong?" she said. "You seem a bit withdrawn."

"Do I? I'm sorry."

We made conversation but I could not avoid thinking about Lawlor. He had no right to be there. A kind of futile indignation was my main reaction. His presence was like a proof of Anna's view that deception would not be possible. At any moment he could have sat on a chair beside us and I suppose that I would have had to fight him or commence a series of lies that would have fallen apart when he went back with her to her room. What's he doing here? I asked myself again and again as if my memory contained an answer that could be reawakened by this repetition. If he had come to Amsterdam to search for her he would not have been meeting an IRA leader on a houseboat. It was coincidence but that was no consolation. The shadow of future intrigue seemed to fall across the table between us, and because she was unaware of it I found myself looking at her with unreasonable dislike. She was talking about someone whom she had met in the Rijksmuseum, a man from Rotterdam who had, with enormous, old-fashioned civility, suggested that they go to bed.

"He was about forty-five," she said, "with a walrus moustache and a pair of rimless glasses. I could hardly believe what he was saying. He seemed so reserved and polite. She attempted to imitate his accent. " 'It would please me very much if you would sleep with me. Let me tell you also that I have great skill and much experience. Your time will not be wasted.' I wish you had seen him."

"I would have," I said to her irritably, "if you didn't go off by yourself every morning."

"But you didn't mind," she said. "It gave us both freedom. What's the matter? Please, let's not fight."

"I don't know," I said. "I'm just feeling . . . jumpy," and for a moment I was tempted to tell her. "It must be because there's so little time left."

"I know what you mean," she said, accepting this poor explanation with marked relief. "This time tomorrow we'll be what? On the plane? But still, we have almost twenty-four hours left. Let's make the most of them. I bought you a present." She took a small parcel from her bag and left it on the table. I unwrapped the tissue paper, embarrassed because I had nothing to give her in return, and found a miniature porcelain figure of an owl that I had admired in some shop that we had visited.

"I hope you don't think that he's silly."

"I think that he's beautiful," I said.

"The owl seems to be some kind of symbol here. You see him all over the city. Keep him as a talisman, so that he'll always remind you."

"I won't need anything to remind me."

"Keep him safe all the same," she said.

It stood on my table until three or four weeks ago, when, pushing some papers aside, I knocked it to the floor. I picked up the tiny pieces and almost wept.

"I'm buying your present in the morning."

"You mustn't feel you have to," she said. "It's got to be something small. I know that you haven't much money left."

She bought us two bottles of Skol and I was glad that I had not been foolish enough to tell her. It was coincidence; nothing more.

"I'd like to have the opportunity to travel more often," I said. "Does Peter get around much?"

"Not a lot. He goes to London now and then if there's a big Press conference but that's about all."

"Has he ever been here?" I asked, unable to resist the peripheries of danger. It was a little like telling her without the inevitable damage of her reaction.

"No. Why do you ask?"

"I just wondered."

"I posted him a card this morning."

"What did you write on it? Wish you were here?"

She looked offended and then I saw with surprise that she was blushing.

"That was a joke," I said.

"I know. It's just that I can't really feel funny about it." The blush faded quickly. "I wish that I could be in love without deception. I don't want to be destructive."

We were moving back towards the old path of conversation.

"We've been over that before," I said, too abruptly, for she put down her glass with a force that was intended to indicate resentment.

"Are we only to talk about things that you suggest? Am I censored . . . ?"

"Remember what you said about fighting."

"All the same," she said, "I don't like being cut off in the middle of a sentence. It just makes things worse. It adds to the tension."

I knew that Lawlor's presence in Amsterdam was indirectly responsible for the way that we were talking. Deceit was even more damaging than she feared. I still looked anxiously at the people who were passing as we started to undo the damage and reassure each other of the value of love. The owl was beside my glass. I pushed it across the table towards her.

"You can make a wish on it," I said. "A new superstition that I've just created, but one that actually works."

She put her finger on the small, jutting yellow beak.

"What did you wish?"

"I can't tell you. That breaks the magic. Now it's your turn."

"I don't know what to wish."

"Whatever you want most," she said emphatically as if she believed that there might be some secret power behind the pretence.

"All right."

I remember wishing that Lawlor were dead. I took the owl in my hand and she smiled across at me, innocently. I put it down on the table feeling vaguely ashamed.

"I hope that your wish comes true."

"Let's have one more drink," I said, "then decide what we're going to do."

We spent the afternoon in the Rijksmuseum. I was happy to be there, remembering that Lawlor had no real interest in painting. The entrance was crowded; American tourists seemed to be staging a small revolt. Someone was missing. "You can't let her out of your sight," a woman said with heavy resignation. "Let's each take a different room and meet here in ten minutes. I'll go back to that nightwatch thing and somebody better check the john." She hustled them into action, a brooch shining on her massive chest like a military medal.

"I wouldn't like to be whoever it is," Anna said as we went up the stairs, behind the inevitable party of small baffled Japanese. "How can they ever lose a war?"

"They leave the women at home."

"Think of how she could affect the balance of power."

We went to rooms that neither of us had seen before. I remember that we both liked a bronze statue of the god Siva dancing within a ring of fire, the seven sacred rivers of India in his hair.

"Are you religious?" she asked me.

"Sometimes."

"What kind of times?"

"When I'm lonely. And you?"

"I'd like to be. I try to be some of the time but not when I'm lonely. When I'm happy."

"Are you feeling religious now?"

"No, it isn't a feeling, is it? It's an aspiration. I certainly believe in life after death and the possibility of some kind of new awareness. Looking at that statue somehow reminds me that that's what I want. When God exists like a new idea."

"And sin is what?" I asked her as we went to another room and looked at T'ang horses. A small girl ran noisily past us, shouting in excited German, and the voice of a guide came from some distant corridor. For a few minutes we were left alone in the room.

"A refusal to accept the new idea. Culpable ignorance," she said.

The term brought back memories of catechism classes and complex fears. I was taught to believe in Christ crucified; the angular, infinitely tragic figure half falling from the cross to which, unwittingly, I had nailed him. The possibility of revenge had seemed all too probable and for many years I believed in a God who, aware of my culpable ignorance, waited to knock on the door like a secret policeman. The idea of love came much later and could never be completely detached from a sense of hostile observation.

"Does that sound too glib?"

"Not at all."

"I suppose the worst characteristic of my religion", she said, "is that it embarrasses me, always, to talk about it."

"It's one's private business."

"Not entirely. It's just that I haven't got a vocabulary to say things meaningfully without sounding pious or pretentious. And you look embarrassed."

"Not by what you're saying. It's because of how little I have to say in reply."

"Then you know what I mean?"

"It's not the same," I said. "I'm missing more than a vocabulary."

"When I love you," she said, "I hurt Peter. He doesn't know about it now but that's not the point. He's still being hurt. I think that the worst sin in the situation would be not to realise that. To be quite indifferent to the consequences of an action."

"Is awareness enough?"

"It's a start," she said. I thought of Lawlor standing in the cabin doorway and my wish on the owl that she had chosen for me with love.

"What will we look at next?" I asked her.

We went from room to room. As the afternoon went by the possibility of meeting Lawlor seemed increasingly remote. I began to enjoy being with her and listening to the answers that she gave to my questions about paintings. I had read Vasari not long before and remembered some eccentric details from the lives of artists; Paolo Uccello revolting against the cheese diet of the Abbot of San Miniato and Fra Filippo Lippi coping with his remarkable lust.

She did not like Van Scorel's Mary Magdalene but the ambiguity in the face appealed to me; it might have been hesitation or sultry defiance. We argued about it, laughing. The afternoon was a sudden success and when she said that she had made a plan for the evening I waited to hear it with some of the excitement of a child.

"First we have dinner in the Dorrius Restaurant where you're going to get just a little bit drunk. Then, without wasting any time, we go back to the hotel . . ."

"That's an excellent plan."

"You think so? I'm going to cry tomorrow when we have to go."

"It isn't an ending," I said.

"I know, but I feel safe here. I can't imagine a nicer context."

When we came out of the Dorrius Restaurant she said that she wanted to walk to the hotel. It was a bright evening and, as usual, we paused in Leidsestraat to listen to the barrel-organ.

"Rituals", she said, "must be observed."

We were waiting for a tram to pass, holding hands when she said, "This is going to be the nicest evening."

The tram went past and Lawlor stared out at us. For a few seconds his face seemed to be directly opposite mine, then the tram went on and people were coming towards us from across the street. I turned to her. She was looking up at me and I knew that she had not seen him.

"Don't you think so?"

"Think what?"

"Wake up! That this is going to be the nicest evening."

The tram stopped farther up the street but I could not see who got out.

"Michael!" She was shaking my arm.

"I'm sorry darling. Yes, I'm sure that it will be."

I expected to see him running towards us, but when the tram went on the only person standing on the concrete island in the middle of the street was an elderly lady with a shopping bag.

"Why are you brooding?"

"I don't mean to. Let's get back."

Would he be in the hotel? I went nervously into the foyer almost hoping to see him there, for whatever happened could not be worse than the corrosive effect of suspense.

"No calls?" I said to the girl who gave us our key. She was sucking a stub of pencil that was covered with small, pink bite marks.

"No. No calls. No."

"Who on earth did you think would call?" Anna asked as we went up the narrow stairs past old prints of Amsterdam and a bamboo table on the landing.

"Just in case there was any change in the tickets," I said.

"But they're booked, aren't they?"

"There can still be changes."

"Can there?" she said with surprise. "That's never happened to me. Unless there's a fog or something."

I opened the door of our room and went inside without any anticipation of pleasure. The window had not been closed and insects droned past our faces. I knew that I would have to tell her. There was no possibility now of the discretion of which I had spoken so easily.

She started to undress and, watching her, I decided to wait until the following day. I wanted her. She put her clothes on a chair, and, selfishly, I could not bear the thought of the night passing away in nervous tension. I even attempted to convince myself that he had not seen us although I knew that this could not be true. That night when I finally went to sleep I dreamed of his face floating before me like a lighted Hallowe'en mask, the expression never changing.

"I love you," I said, after we had made love on the ludicrous, creaking bed that she seemed to like.

"It was different that time," she said.

"In what way?"

"I'm not sure. Nice but different."

I was smoking a cigarette, watching the smoke trailing and dissolving above her body. I wondered if I had brought some kind of finality to the act. She reached out and put her hand on my shoulder, gently, like a gesture of reassurance, and said, "It was the nicest."

I could not think of a reply. A board in the ceiling creaked and a pigeon outside the window made soft lascivious noises.

"Can we ever come back here again?"

"We must," I said without any conviction. I remember her puzzled eyes, a slight frown, her hand brushing damp hair back from her forehead.

"Is something wrong?"

I should have told her then but I did not.

"No, nothing is wrong," I said.

"That's not true. You've been kind of . . . abstracted since dinner. What's . . . ?"

"Please, Anna. I've told you that there's nothing wrong."

"This was supposed to be our special evening," she said.

"Have I spoiled it for you?"

"Something seems to have spoiled it for you," she said bitterly, covering herself with a blanket and turning away from me. Hostility lay between us like a blade. I want to marry her, I thought, casting Lawlor in an easy image of the destroyer. How often do we blame ourselves for our own unhappiness or search out our own mistakes? Her shoulders were shaking, and when I forced her to turn her face was blotched with tears.

"It's foolish to look forward to anything," she said. "It just invites things to go wrong. You change too much. Why couldn't we just be happy here?"

"But I was."

"You can't speak so brusquely . . ."

"I didn't mean to, Anna. The whole evening wasn't like that."

"No, but after we'd made love and I said that it was the nicest. Can't you guess how ashamed I feel when it doesn't seem to matter to you?"

"It mattered a great deal."

"No one would believe it."

"I just don't want to lose you," I said.

"Is that the truth?"

"Completely."

We lay silently beside each other like effigies in a museum. The pigeon moaned restlessly.

"You'll see me in Dublin?"

"As often as you like," she said.

"Despite what you said about the furtiveness?"

"I'm sure that I exaggerated the importance of that. The worst thing will probably be the contrast with here, and that can't last for long."

She went to sleep before I did, her head resting uncomfortably on a stretched-out arm. I lay listening to her breathing. When I touched her cheek she did not wake but I must have entered her dream for she said, "No, over there. Near the corner."

I bent close to her face and saw that she was smiling.

I went from shop to shop, looking for a gift and expecting to encounter Lawlor. The sky was overcast; it had rained earlier and some drops were still falling from shop awnings. In Kalverstraat I thought that I saw him but when the man turned, he was older and looked more sardonic. I had a cup of coffee, then with no time left for more searching, I bought a book of Van Gogh reproductions and went back to the hotel. We had packed before breakfast. The suitcases were in the foyer. Anna turned when I went into the bedroom.

"I was getting worried about you," she said. "I've ordered a taxi."

I gave her the parcel.

"Don't bother looking at it now. I'm afraid it's not very original."

I went through the morose ritual of opening drawers and checking the wardrobe shelves.

"I think that we've got everything," I said, aware of how much we were leaving in that room.

"It was lovely," she said. She was wearing an overcoat that I had not seen before and I felt tenderness towards her, knowing that her happiness concealed a sense of loss.

"I'm sorry for anything that disappointed you," I said. "And especially for last night."

"That was only a few minutes."

I put my arms around her.

"Are you sure?"

"Yes, certain. When I go home," she said, "the first painting I do will be for you. Then you'll give me the one that you have. Isn't that agreed?"

"If you say so."

"Then it's agreed." She went to the window. "We'll see the taxi arrive."

I sat on the unmade bed and watched her. It would be easy to understand love if one's emotions were geometric; line reading on to line making logical patterns of feeling. She turned and smiled at me, a moment that I remember with complete clarity, then she turned away and I find it more difficult to recall my feelings. The guilt was starting then. I should have told her that Lawlor had seen us; because I had not done so there was some aggression in the way that I considered breaking the news when we got back to Dublin. He could, after all, be waiting for her in their flat.

"All right," she said. "There's the taxi."

Chapter Twelve

When I told her, in the cold, damp living-room of my flat, she stared across at me as if I were speaking a foreign language. There was no comprehension on her face. She had taken a book from the shelves; she placed it slowly on the table.

"I didn't tell you before," I said, not looking at her. "I didn't want to spoil . . ."

"Are you certain it was Peter?"

"I'm afraid so. I saw him twice. On a houseboat and then last night when we were crossing Leidsestraat, he passed by in a tram."

"On a houseboat?" she said incredulously. "What was he doing on a houseboat?"

"How would I know?"

"On a houseboat! You must be mistaken."

"I wish that I were. Anyway, there was no doubt about it last night. I saw him clearly. And he saw us," I added unnecessarily. Her reaction was far too vague. I wanted to provoke the reality of her feelings and discover their implications for me.

"Why are you doing this?" she asked me calmly. "He wasn't in Amsterdam."

"For Christ's sake!" I said. "I'm telling you that I saw him! Why the hell would I make it up?"

"That's what I'm trying to understand."

"Anna!"

I went across to her and attempted to take her hands, but she pulled them away from me.

"I don't know yet why you're inventing it," she said.

"I'm not inventing it! I wish that it weren't true. It's the worst luck in the world."

"You'd have told me at the time," she said, but some doubt had come into her voice.

"I didn't want to spoil everything. Anyway, he didn't see me the first time so it wouldn't have mattered."

"But he knew that I'd be in Amsterdam," she said. "He'd have told me."

"Maybe he had some reason . . ."

"What reason?"

"I don't know."

"There couldn't be any reason."

"I'd like to pretend as well," I said, "but what's the point? You might as well face the fact."

"I'm going to phone his office."

"Are you sure that you should at this stage?"

"May I use your phone?"

"Yes, of course."

"Would you mind leaving me alone?"

I went resentfully into the bedroom. I had left the bed unmade and over the week the room had become squalid. There was dust on the glass of her painting. I brushed it away with my fingers, then went to the window. An ambulance turned in from Clyde Road and accelerated towards Baggot Street, its siren wailing. I could hear the sound of her voice coming through the wall, as I waited, my resentment growing more deep. When she called me, I went back to the living-room like a prisoner returning to hear a verdict.

"He has ten days' leave," she said. "He won't be back until the day after tomorrow. They don't know where he's gone."

Her hand was resting on the telephone as if she were waiting for some prearranged signal.

"You should have told me," she said.

"I decided against it."

"You should have told me. It was wrong. And last night. The special night! You shouldn't have just pretended..."

"I didn't want to spoil it."

"But you spoiled it anyway!" she said.

"Now you know why."

I wanted to find some constructive initiative before we moved even further away from each other. I could see a nerve beating at the side of her face and her knuckles became startlingly white against the telephone.

"Anna..." I said. "I'll try to explain."

"There's no point now."

"You don't even know what I want to say."

"Can you even start to imagine what it's like for me?" she said.

"It isn't the end of the world."

"You don't care. So it isn't the start or the end of anything for you."

"But he doesn't love you."

"Yes he does. Don't try to tell me about my private life. I ought to know."

We stood facing each other like boxers waiting for the bell.

"I don't know what I'm going to do," she said.

"I want to marry you."

"Don't say that!"

"I want to marry you," I said again with a sudden escapist vision of peaceful days in some new flat, her easel in one room, our lovemaking punctuating the days as swings of boredom and depression had so often punctuated them in the past.

"I'm not going to do it to him," she said.

"You love me," I said, "so you can't simply do it to me."

"You said we could be happy together without anyone knowing." She sounded like a child from whom the prospect of a treat has been taken away. I held her, rigid, in my arms.

"Just remember what I said when you're deciding what to do."

Her tension was like a positive force against me. It seemed to creep through my arms like the onset of some disease, and when I tried to kiss her our faces bumped foolishly together.

"I'm going home."

"I'll leave you there."

"No," she said, pushing me away. "I don't want that. I want to go there by myself. If you had told me we could have been prepared for this."

"Hardly."

"Yes," she said. "Yes, we could. There wouldn't have been such a sense of retrospective deceit. When you made love to me last night some part of your mind must have been detached and speculative. You were only using me. That isn't making love." The anger that I felt must have shown on my face for she took a step backwards as if fearing a blow.

"It wasn't like that," I said lamely, unable to prove that she was wrong.

"I'm going home."

"Your case is in the car."

We went downstairs. In the hallway, I pushed her against the wall and said, "You love me!" It sounded like a threat. She stared at me, a little frightened, and lifted her hand to protect her face.

"Don't you?"

"I think so," she said. "But that doesn't solve anything now. I've got to think what I'm going to do. And I've got to talk to Peter."

We moved apart as the front door opened and Mrs Towers came into the hall. When she saw us she paused, then said, "Oh, you're back Mr Waldron. I'm so glad. I've been living here alone. The other tenants are away."

She went slowly up the stairs and we stood there, waiting for her door to close.

"I can't talk now," Anna said.

"I'm sorry that I didn't tell you before."

"All right. I might have done the same." She attempted to smile. "If I over-reacted I'm sorry too. But I don't want to talk anymore. We'd come to the wrong conclusions. It isn't the time."

"When will I see you?"

"I'll phone you when I've thought things out."

"That's not very satisfactory for me," I said, unable to conceal the annoyance and the self-pity in my voice. Sometimes I see myself in the future, alone like Mrs Towers, depending on the casual interest of acquaintances. The sound of her out-of-tune piano came crazily down the stairs.

"Stop thinking about yourself," Anna said, so unexpectedly that I almost laughed with embarrassment.

"I'm only too willing to think about you if you wouldn't insist on blocking me out. And I'm willing to talk to Lawlor..."

She opened the front door. Someone was mowing a lawn and the smell of grass came like a memory of innocence. She insisted on walking. I took her suitcase from the car and attempted again to persuade her to let me drive her but she refused. I watched her go out through the gate, the suitcase in her hand dragging down one shoulder as she walked slowly away.

Late that evening the telephone rang. I answered it but nobody spoke. I heard the hiss and hum of an open line. "Hello!" I repeated the number. A click was followed by the dialling tone. I put back the receiver knowing that there would be another call. I waited for twenty minutes and the bell seemed startlingly loud. "Hello! Press button A," I said, but nothing happened. Faint snatches of some conversation on another line were all that I could hear. "Hello." The click was oddly final as if it were the negative ending of a long conversation. When the telephone rang again I did not answer it. I went from room to room and the sound pursued me. Then I thought that it might be Anna. I ran to the living-room but when I got there the ringing stopped. When I dialled her number it was engaged.

I watched the end of a play on television; the comic side of adultery with two men and a woman getting together at dinner to talk things out in a civilised way. The inept husband and the alcoholic lover were old schoolfriends. They recalled bad schoolboy jokes as the wife watched resignedly.

I answered the telephone.

"Look, what do you want?" I said. The click came abruptly. I poured myself a whiskey and waited. There were three more calls. I swore pointlessly down the line and heard breathing.

"Is that you, Lawlor?"

I waited anxiously for an answer.

"Look, I know that it's you," I said. The silence was unnerving. "Why don't you answer? I'll talk. I want to meet you," I said, and the click was like a premonition of despair. I sat watching the telephone, willing it not to ring as the time went slowly by. It must have been him, I thought, and now that he knows that I know he won't call again. The telephone rang as if to make nonsense of my theory. I lifted the receiver but said nothing, aware now that my reaction could be provoking further calls. I stood for some minutes, listening. It was like a battle of wills and I lost. I slammed down the receiver and went out. It was dark and becoming cold.

I had a drink in Searson's, hoping to meet someone whom I knew. The jocularity of strangers depressed me. I walked down to Percy Place. A prostitute in a yellow dress, a fur stole across her shoulders, stepped out from behind a tree. A middle-aged man followed her, buttoning his trousers and hurrying away across the bridge. I walked along by the canal. The water was still and the reflection of lights were blurs beneath its surface.

I remember thinking bitterly that the familiar pattern was starting again. I'll soon be standing outside her flat, I thought, to see if there's a light in the window.

"Excuse me."

The old man's face looked hopelessly up at me. He was sprawling in the grass, a bottle of cheap sherry in his hand.

"I could still get to the Iveagh," he said, "if I had a few more pence." The hopeless face broke into a stark, fixed grin. "Just a few more pence."

I gave him the change that was in my pocket, feeling guilty and ashamed. His predicament was so much worse than mine that I resented its impingement.

"Bugger you!" he said, still grinning. The money slid between his fingers on to the grass. "Who the hell do you think you are?" I could hear his choking laughter following me as I went back to my flat.

The telephone was ringing. I hurried up the last flight of stairs and answered it, speaking involuntarily.

"Hello."

The silence was deeply humiliating. I felt helpless and inept.

"Hello, what is this? What do you want?" I almost appealed to the silence. "What do you want?" I stood there waiting for the click, and the silence went on like a scarcely tolerable noise. I had not switched on the light; the shapes of objects in the room seemed unfamiliar.

"I'm going to hang up," I said. There was no reaction to this threat. I put back the receiver. When I switched on the light the room regained its reassuring familiarity. I dialled Anna's number. The high-pitched engaged sound came mockingly along the line. I could hear Mrs Towers performing a nightly security ritual in her flat; the windows being fastened, bolts being slid across on doors.

I had another whiskey and watched the telephone. I did not want to leave it off the hook in case Anna attempted to call me. The room was cold and when I started to read a biography of Parnell, from which I had been taking notes, my concentration flagged after a few pages. "Bad reception in Galway — whiggery," I wrote on a piece of paper, then stared across at the telephone like someone at a séance waiting for the table to move.

There was one more call. I lifted the receiver and waited, hopelessly, for Anna's voice. I could hear distinct breathing then a snatch of music and the sound of door being slammed.

"Hello."

There was no answer. "This is absolutely ridiculous," I said with a calmness that I did not feel. The temptation to shout out abuse was almost irresistible. "Can't you play the game with somebody else?" The click was like a gesture of derision. I left the receiver off the hook and went into the cheerless bedroom; the unpacked case lying on the unmade bed. I slept badly and woke when pale, grey light was brightening the room. I remember the feeling of resignation with which I put the receiver back on to the hook and waited.

Her voice was like a reprieve. I had answered the telephone anticipating silence.

"Are you there? It's me," she said. "We needn't have

worried."

"How do you mean?"

"Can I meet you?"

"Of course," I said. "Have you spoken . . ."

"I'll tell you when I see you. Could we meet in the Hibernian? I'll be there in half an hour."

I arrived before her. The lounge was almost empty. I read a magazine until she came in, carrying her suitcase.

"Have you not been home?"

"Yes, last night."

Her tentative smile made me feel uneasy.

"Well, tell me about it," I said.

"I tried to get you on the phone last night but there was no answer."

"The one call that I missed?" I said bitterly. "Your phone was engaged whenever I tried."

"I left it off the hook. I didn't want to talk to anyone after Peter called."

"He called you?"

"From Belfast," she said. "He's been on leave all right but he never left Belfast. He was doing some research for articles that he might sell in America."

"Anna," I said. "I saw him. Not once but twice. I can absolutely assure you."

"He ought to know where he's been!"

"As I'm sure that he does. If he wants to say that he was in Belfast all the time that's fine by me but it simply isn't the truth."

"You seem to *want* him to have seen us."

"I just know that he did," I said, tired at having to be so insistent. "What exactly did he say?"

"He asked me how I enjoyed Amsterdam and I said very much, and then he said that he'd like to go there some time. He said that we must go together and I could show him around. So I knew, then, that he hadn't been there and I asked him what he had done and he told me about the research. Then I was certain that he didn't know anything. He was in particularly good form."

She seemed to be excited as well as relieved and more self-confident than I could remember having seen her. I knew that nothing would convince her that Lawlor was lying.

"All right," I said, "if that's the way that you think it is."

"Will you never give in?" she said. "Do you think that we'd have had the kind of conversation that we had if he knew or even suspected? When he came on the phone first I was actually afraid of him."

"All right. What happens next?" I asked.

"That's why I wanted to see you."

She pulled her chair nearer to the table and I felt both love and desire as I thought of her, alone, making plans in which I was included. I had ordered drinks for us. The waiter brought them and we sat, suspended in silence, waiting for him to go.

"He asked me to come up to Belfast for a few days. I'm taking the train," she said. "The school opens soon and I won't be so free . . . I want to work things out."

This inferred my exclusion. I felt all the old possessive jealousy start to twist inside me like a rage but must have hidden it for she went on, calmly.

"I hope that you'll understand."

"Understand what?"

I had spoken too loudly. Three women at another table gave up their conversation and looked across at us.

"What I feel," Anna said.

"What *do* you feel?" I said. "It's time that I knew."

"I've always told you as much as I knew myself. I was happy in Amsterdam. You were very good to me," she said, as if I had arranged her travel permit or helped her across a busy street.

"I love you," she said. "If I weren't married to Peter . . . but, you see, I love him as well."

"More than you love me?"

"Differently. Not more, maybe even less. But I can't go on deceiving him and I'm not going to say that our marriage is a failure until we've made real efforts at turning it into a success."

"That's splendid!"

"Please try to understand," she said. "I've got more confidence now. It's possible that he doesn't love me and if so I've lost both of you, but that's the chance that I've got to take."

"And we . . ."

"Can't we be friends?" she said. "I know it's a cliché, but can't we?" She had not tasted her drink. She took the glass in her hands and stared into it as if expecting to see some glimpse of the future forming amongst the ice.

"I don't know," I said. "Friendship is more difficult than love. I've never had much talent for it. I never know what's expected from me or what I want to give."

"Affection."

"That's always part of something else. Like sex. I want you," I said. "Even now I want you."

"I'm not good material for the deception of an affair. Call it old-fashioned morality or cowardice or both or whatever you like."

"I won't call it anything," I said. "You're a free agent."

"That's the only thing that I'm not."

"Although your marriage has no validity?"

"That's only from one point of view," she said with a show of patience. "I wish it were different. I'm not a person who likes conflict. I didn't ask you to come to Amsterdam."

"No."

"And although you said that you wanted me to marry you, you know that it isn't what you want."

"I meant it when I asked you."

"I believe that you did," she said.

"And I'd marry you rather than lose you. I know that doesn't sound like the highest degree of positive commitment, but it is for me."

"Then we're not all that different," she said. "You don't think much of my commitment to Peter."

I finished my drink and ordered two more. She looked at her watch and said, "I shouldn't. I'll have to go soon."

"I'm taking you to the station."

"I wouldn't have expected that," she said.

"Just consider one thing. You're not going to accept that Lawlor saw us in Amsterdam but he did. You know him, so, even in theory, you can decide why he'd pretend that he hadn't. If I were you I'd have the answer to that worked out before I reached Belfast."

"You're absolutely indefatigable!"

"Maybe I'm a bad loser," I said.

"But you're not the loser! If you only knew how much you've given me and how much I want to return it in any way except the only way that you've considered up to now. I don't want to lose you either. That's what you don't seem to understand."

"It's not easily understood. If you love him less," I said, "why do you want to stay with him? Is it pity?"

She did not answer and her silence was like a goad that made me go on ruthlessly.

"You must be sorry for him! All the fine expressions of not wanting to hurt him and wanting to be constructive, come down in the end to pity, the most squalid weapon in anybody's armoury. Can you not see how you're fooling yourself and trying to fool me? Do you think there's any connection between pity and love? There isn't. It comes from guilt and pride and it corrodes everything except self-satisfaction." The waiter brought us our drinks and I paid for them. When I looked at her again I saw that she was crying silently, not even moving to brush away the tears. The women at the other table were looking across at us, amusement on their faces. We had brought unexpected light relief to their boredom.

"Have you finished now?" Anna said.

"I suppose so."

"Maybe I deserve it," she said, "and maybe I don't. It really isn't important."

She took a handkerchief from her bag and brushed it ineffectually across her face.

"All right," I said.

I would have been able to cope with her anger more easily. Her sudden calmness seemed to be impenetrable.

"I'll have to go now."

I swallowed my drink.

"You don't have to rush," she said. "I can easily get there by myself."

I took her suitcase.

"I'm taking you to the station."

"I'm sorry to waste the drink."

The book of Van Gogh reproductions was on the back seat of the car.

"Please take it with you," I said. "It's yours. I have the owl."

"I'm delighted to have it," she said.

We did not speak again until we had almost arrived at the station. We drove across Butt Bridge. A dredger came down the Liffey, black smoke trailing from its rusted funnel.

"It's not like Amsterdam," she said.

"Anna, I'm sorry that I made you cry again. If things don't work out for you . . ."

She put her hand on my arm.

"Don't make promises," she said. "I'm tempted to make them as well but they all suppose that time is going to stand still."

"You know where I'll be."

"It's nice of you to say that."

"Nice!" I said, almost angrily. "Nice! It has nothing to do with niceness."

"Then generous."

"Or with generosity either."

I stopped outside the station.

"Don't come in," she said. "I'll manage. Do you really mean it?"

"Yes I do."

"Even though my priority now, for whatever reason, is Peter?"

"Yes. And listen, you're to mind yourself. I'm deeply suspicious of him."

She laughed. I handed her the suitcase.

"No matter what happens we can still be friends?"

"No, friendship is the single thing that we can't have," I said, knowing that of all the things I had said to her in the last half-hour this was the only one of which I was certain. "Anything else you like."

"That's a pity," she said. "I'd like to have thought . . . but it's too uncertain anyway."

I have attempted, often, to remember how she looked then but have always failed. The inflection in her voice comes back to me and I seem to remember her fingers pulling restlessly at the buttons on her coat. I see her walking up the steps and going through the station doorway. She did not look back.

Chapter Thirteen

The manuscript that Burgess had returned to me lay like a blackmail letter on my table. I did some work on it that evening but could not concentrate for long; the comments in the margins depressed me. I began work on it again very early the following morning, determined to finish soon with a plan that had become a tedious chore. I was attempting to draw a clear distinction between Davitt's preoccupation with social justice and the doctrinaire if almost mystical nationalism that was more typical of Irish leaders. The eviction of his family had fixed the idea of security of tenure like an obsession in his mind. Many men are made great by devoting their lives to regaining the losses of their childhood. Greatness, one could argue, depends on the historical relevance of their losses and the methods open to them in their efforts to compensate. I know that it is a mistake to look for contemporary morality in history. Progress has often been forced brutally upon unwilling majorities, yet I admired the distinction that Davitt drew between the need for united action and the enshrined tradition for the unleashing of cyclical violence. When considering Irish history, as it moves through all its tortuous phases, I tend to believe in the ethical superiority of victims. I began to enjoy the work again. I finished a chapter and sketched out the plan for another before anticipating the kind of editorial comment that it might provoke. "More detail on Boycott affair. The name is, after all, a part of the language!" "No need for so much on Devoy." "The origin of the name of New Departure?"

It was almost lunchtime. The owl that she had bought for me was standing on the table. I remembered her putting down a book and staring at me incredulously.

I went out to get a newspaper. It had been raining and a cold breeze stirred the branches of the trees in Herbert Park. I met an acquaintance in the newsagent's.

"What do you think is going to happen in the North?" he asked me. "I used to think that we'd see a solution soon but now I'm not so sure."

Our ritualistic conversation brushed lightly across the surface of the subject.

"It's all so pointless," he said with something like genuine concern, as we left the shop. He blinked at me myopically, scratching the side of his pallid face with a gloved finger. "If it goes on much longer like this I don't see how the violence can be prevented from spreading down here. Once you undermine the democratic institutions of the state the result . . ." He paused and produced the conclusion like the climax of a conjuring trick ". . . is anarchy."

He had formerly supported the Provisional IRA, convinced that they could not be beaten. "In a just cause," I had once heard him saying, "there is no such thing as defeat. Our history is a series of deferred victories!" I would have challenged the subjective basis for his change of mind if the day had not been cold and if thoughts of Anna had not kept intruding like fantasies.

I went back to the flat and opened *The Irish Times*. Her picture was on the front page. I stared at it with surprise before seeing the headline YOUNG ARTIST KILLED IN BOOBY TRAPPED CAR.

Just before ten o'clock on the previous night, she had left the Europa Hotel and travelled with Lawlor, in his car, along the Grosvenor Road, past the Royal Victoria Hospital. They had turned into the Falls Road and I cannot even guess what they might have been saying to each other. Lawlor's grey Volkswagen was recognised by a woman who told the Press that she saw them driving along the Whiterock Road to Ballymurphy.

Lawlor parked the car in a short, residential street and entered the house of a man who was described as a friend but who probably gave or sold him occasional pieces of information. He went into the kitchen while Anna sat waiting for him in the car. After being treated for shock, Lawlor made a statement in which he said that he had told her that he would be back in one or two minutes. When they heard the explosion, he ran with the owner of the house to the front door, the glass panels of which had been shattered and were powdered across the hall. They saw black smoke pouring from the wreckage of the car and there was a piece of metal jammed between the railings of the garden gate.

Lawlor ran towards the car while neighbours came out of their houses and shouted at each other in fear and anger. Somebody telephoned for an ambulance.

A large jagged hole had been blown in the roof of the car and the covering of the seats was on fire. Lawlor attempted to pull open the passenger door but it was jammed and he fell to his knees as he breathed in the thick black smoke. A man dragged him away, saying, "There's nobody in it," for he could see nothing except the burning seats. When he heard Lawlor saying "My wife" he looked again. The smoke was clearing and on the floor, lying across the clutch and the accelerator, he saw a blackened human leg. There was almost nothing else there, but behind the car a woman saw what at first she took to be a small animal that had been killed in the explosion. When she went near to it she screamed and was sick, staring at it as vomit poured down over her chin. Two neighbours helped her away but the sound of her screams could be heard throbbing from the house. The man who had dragged Lawlor away from the car held him as he struggled, looking around in the hope that someone could advise him on what should be done next. He was a strong man but when Lawlor's elbow caught him on the chest, he released his grip and moved back from the burning car.

Lawlor's face was blackened from the smoke. He stood apart from the people who felt an indefinable fear of him, as if contact could bring more tragedy to their street. He made one more attempt to open the door of the car then went, quietly, with his friend, into the house.

An army patrol arrived, followed by an ambulance and a fire engine. They directed lights into the gardens and the streets and men with plastic bags searched, stooping close to the ground, for anything that they could find. A second ambulance took the screaming woman away.

It was calculated that the amount of explosive used had not been large. Most of the windows along the street were shattered and there was a hole in the garden wall beside which the car had been parked. A piece of the roof had been flung through the window of a house but as the room was empty at the time, the only damage done had been to the furniture. Two children, sleeping near to the window of another of the houses, had their faces cut by broken glass. One, because of the depth of the cuts, was taken away to hospital. The other was treated by the local doctor. Had the bomb been bigger, a British army major was quoted as saying, the number of lives that could have been lost in so confined an area was virtually incalculable. The occupant of the car had had no chance but it was fortunate that nobody else had been passing at the time. "Whoever set the timing device on this booby trap", he said, "had, of course, no idea where the car would be when the bomb went off. That's what makes this kind of thing particularly vicious."

I pieced this account together from the newspapers that I read and from the radio. I spent all of the day searching for any other detail that would add to what I already knew. In one of the evening papers there was a short appreciation of her work as a painter and a picture of her mother, a small bewildered looking woman showing none of the confidence that Anna had described, posed uneasily outside the door of a farmhouse. In the appreciation, her potential was recognised. "As she gained in technical confidence she would without question have become one of our most important artists. Her growth between exhibitions was both marked and impressive. Some of her most accomplished work will remain to remind us of how much we have lost."

It was later in the day before I began to experience grief. The pursuit of information had made her abstract. I fitted fact to fact as if I were sketching out a new chapter for my book. I know now that I was warding off the guilt that began to grow later amongst the complex sources of my grief, like another person insisting on making judgements on facts and passing a final verdict. I thought of her in Amsterdam, sitting alone at a café table and looking up to say, slowly, "You?" She would have been alive if I had not followed her with my imperfect offer of love.

At first, I was reluctant to consider the motive behind her death. My suspicions seemed too unlikely, yet they persisted and grew as a counterpoint to grief and as a part of my self-accusation. Nobody claimed responsibility for the bomb. It seemed to be an isolated incident; there were no other violent happenings in Belfast on that day. Commentators surmised that the choice of car had been deliberate; that one of the paramilitary organisations was taking revenge on Lawlor for something that he had written. It was his body, they assumed, that should have been scattered across the suburban street. Other journalists had been threatened yet this was the first time that violence had been used against one. "No, I think it more likely", a colleague of Lawlor's said on the television news, "that it was the work of an individual with a grudge and would not have had the sanction of whatever organisation he belongs to. I very much doubt that any claim of responsibility will be made. To be perfectly frank, a claim would be highly counter-productive."

An individual with a grudge; the phrase twisted through my mind like a long-suppressed memory coming painfully to the surface.

I went out for a walk. The streets seemed to be redolent with discontent. I seldom noticed them when I was happy but now they became, as before, the landscape of sadness and revenge. Shadows mourned on the pavements and when I came to Barbara's flat I found myself standing at the gate and staring at a line of light between the curtains of her window. She was the only person I knew to whom it might be possible to explain all that had happened. I do not know for how long I stood there, indecisive and cold. I moved on only when I heard a hall door being slammed and footsteps crunching on the gravel path of an adjoining house.

I became convinced that he had killed her. He had seen us in Amsterdam; it was he who had made the telephone calls to my flat; he had asked her to come to Belfast. She had gone with some hope of a constructive future to meet the finality of his revenge. I built up evidence against him in my mind as I walked along Leeson Street. Somebody waved to me from a car but I did not recognise the face.

I went back to my flat and spent most of the night thinking about it, getting drunk as dawn light came gradually into the room and shedding tears that may, I must confess, have had more to do with pity for myself than with grief for her. I began to comprehend his motives. He had never possessed her. Their love was partitioned by a farcical indignity. All of his pride must have been dependent on her belief in his capacity to love her, and perhaps he thought that I had taken that away. I had certainly attempted to do so and he could not have known that I had failed. He must have grown desperate as her love made a constant demand on him that he could not answer. A belief in the future had depended on separation until I had unleashed the violence that had grown, disguised as hope and love between them. Like a man placing a bomb in a busy street, his action had more to do with an impotent inability to change the present than with any hope of influencing the future.

I imagined them leaving the hotel. He would not have told her that he had seen us in Amsterdam. There would have been no warning. She may have smiled secretly at this confirmation of my stubbornly believed mistake. The explosive was somewhere beneath the car so he would have driven slowly and carefully, looking into the driving mirror in the fear that some other motorist would not put on their brakes in time and crash into the back of the car. There was probably some defensiveness in their conversation. They had not seen each other for some weeks. He may have asked her about the exhibition, or perhaps she told him about the paintings that she had seen in the Rijksmuseum, or the café that she had discovered in the Spui. They may even have fought, but I doubted it. In my imagination the very worst thing about that journey was its appearance of normality. He parked in the quiet street, saying that he would be back in a minute or two. Before leaving the car he must have pressed some switch or pulled some cord that set a timing device into short action. Did he look at her then, knowing that his feeling of inadequacy would soon be ended, that in a few minutes his pride would again be intact? She sat there waiting for him as he, in the house, stood waiting for the sound of revenge.

It was scarcely credible but I believed it. I remember walking around the flat, going from room to room without any purpose. It was a cold morning; the desultory birdsong from the garden was as cheerless as a keen. I made some coffee and when I drank it I began to feel sober and ashamed of my self-pity. I telephoned his Belfast office but hung up before the call was answered. I did not know what I would have said if he had been there. I sat and brooded on the idea of revenge. I had no evidence against him but for at least an hour I was intent on the idea of contacting the Belfast police and making an anonymous accusation. I attempted to hate him but even at the worst moments I realised that the wrong I had done to him was greater than anything that he had done to me.

Chapter Fourteen

I felt totally responsible for her death; good moments that we had shared became, in retrospect, mere preludes to destruction. Guilt buried my grief. I am ashamed of my feelings then as I retreated into myself like a city under siege, hiding from the truth. The day went on like a sentence of waiting. The telephone rang but I did not answer it and my thoughts about her grew maudlin. It occurs to me only now that this is a record of self-deception, of the escapism that lay behind so many of my reactions. In these aberrations from the truth, one glimpses the real level of farce, the hollow formality of relationships that are centred in a desire to be different.

In the evening, while I was walking along Baggot Street, full of self-pity because no one was aware of my loss, I met John Reynolds. He was a sub-editor on Lawlor's newspaper and the author of a small-town novel that had once brought him local fame. We went into Doheny and Nesbitts for a drink, and although he was a pedantic bore I was grateful for his company.

"Yes, my new book is almost finished," he said as if I had enquired about it. "Twelve years' gestation, but worth it in my opinion. It's a panoramic view of contemporary Dublin, a look at the middle classes. I manage to find the peasant that's locked away in the boot of every Mercedes or kept in the bedroom wardrobe."

"That's an interesting thought."

"Yes, it is," he said. "It's an interesting book. This country needs it." He banged his glass on the counter as if about to make a belligerent remark but lapsed into silence and stared at the breasts of a girl who was standing beside us.

"You've almost finished it?" I asked out of a sense of duty, although it was commonly believed that his work on the book had not gone beyond the first few pages.

"A matter of semi-colons. Small curlicues of style."

"That's excellent."

"Yes, it is," he said. "And I'll tell you another thing about it. Apart from its literary merit, as a social document it's absolute dynamite." He might have been repeating a blurb. "In the last section, it exposes involvement of Dublin businessmen with the Provos. All the bombs going off in convenient places. All the property and insurance deals. The whole bloody racket that keeps the violence going on, because there's money in it."

"That was sad about Lawlor's wife," I said. "Did you know her?"

"Yes, I met her," he said. "A rather shadowy woman. She made no great impression on me."

"I didn't know her," I said. That unnecessary lie was almost certainly the most cowardly that I have ever told. I looked away as if expecting him to challenge me. The bar was crowded with people who did not care and I wished that I were at home.

"It was a near thing for Lawlor," he said. "They very nearly got him."

"You think it was meant for him?"

"I know that it was," he said. I wanted to believe it so much that I was almost afraid to ask him how he could be certain.

"Everyone knows", he said, "about the way the fool got himself involved."

"Everyone but me apparently."

"It's common knowledge."

"What is?"

"His involvement with the Provos."

"He seemed to have good contacts," I said. "His reports..."

"Too good. That's how it all started." He laughed and looked preoccupied. He was not going to give away any information unless I asked a direct question. He ordered us drinks and his sense of self-importance was almost palpable. I waited as he counted out his change.

"What way did he get involved?"

"Up to his bloody neck. He began as a sympathiser. That was always in his reports. Then he started doing business with them. The bloody fool couldn't see how he was being used. I tackled him about it two months ago but he couldn't see it. They had flattered him so much. He's not the only one either, I can tell you."

He loosened his tie and looked around the bar as if seeking a more important audience.

"What happened?"

"He went to Amsterdam to buy arms."

"Did he really?" I said with a pretence at surprise.

"And bungled it or changed his mind or something. He came back before the others and locked himself in his flat. Then he started swaggering around in the Europa and dropping hints."

"You don't know why he came home?"

"Not yet," he said with some reluctance. "But it'll come out in the end. He's a talker. He's been transferred from Belfast to here and he's not the sort who can shut up."

"And you think they were after him?"

"Everyone knows that they were," he said, laughing, as if he had made a joke. "He shouldn't have been there in the first place, but to fly back without telling anyone! That's looking for trouble. He could have blown whatever arms deal they were making. He obviously lost his nerve."

The reprieve had not lasted for long. I remember his voice going on like a radio out of tune for I did not understand the words. Lawlor might not have killed her but I was still responsible. I knew why he had come home.

I knocked at the door of Barbara's flat and waited apprehesively. It was very cold. I remember practising the words that I intended to use. "I hate you," I whispered. "I hate you!" She opened the door and said, "Good God. You're the last person I expected to see."

"Am I?" I said foolishly. "Is Margaret at home?"

"She doesn't live here any more. Was it her that you came to see?"

"No. I just wondered. I don't think I'd like to meet her again."

"Are you drunk?"

"Perhaps a little."

"Well, come in," she said.

"No, I won't. I just called to tell you something."

"It's warmer inside."

She put her hand on my arm and the words that I had practised were impossible to say. She was wearing a dressing-gown that was loosely tied; the hint of her breasts reminded me of too many mornings.

"You're not ill or anything?"

"No. Just a little drunk," I said.

"What did you want to tell me?"

"I forget."

"It's cold out here," she said.

"You wouldn't believe what's happened!"

"To you?"

"In a way."

"Come in and tell me. I'll make us coffee."

"No, I won't. I've remembered what I wanted to tell you," I said and the half-conceived expression of hate was beating around in my mind like a new obsession. "It wasn't your fault."

"Well, that's nice to hear," she said, humouring me. I turned and went down the path.

"Michael!"

I waited at the gate.

"Ring me when you're feeling better."

"I'll probably do that," I said.

"For old times' sake."

"Exactly."

"All right," she said.

I went home. The sound of the out-of-tune piano mourned through the house, and a letter from Burgess pointed out new inadequacies in my thinking. I attempted to work out the history of her death but like my outline of Davitt's life it was too uncertain. I did not even know against whom I should wish to take revenge. That was the start of the months of confusion and guilt when I scattered blame around me like a camouflage and crouched for safety in the middle of pretence. I still do not know why she died but now I seldom ask myself the question. The corrupting power of routine has made the answer seem less important.